THE BOOKES OF BABYLON

By

Hollis Phillips

WGWPublishing.com

ISBN: 9798990488939
Printed in the United States
WGW Publishing Inc.
Rochester, NY 14619
wgibbs@wgwpublishing.com

For my mother and father who cultivated in me the courageous will to fight, Sensei who helped synergize my brute rages, and my gracious friends, who nurtured the wisdom to forgive

CHAPTER 1
VARMINTS INVERITUS

> *If death still wants me, **it** is facing a bad victim! I and my twin were born dead on a Friday the 13th -- not breathing at all-- (no kidding.) I revived from **it** with a mind like few others. I willed myself away from **its** darkness, at birth. I had to; my twin didn't. I was born with the painful wisdom of old people, who know too much about the end of life. Even now, I 'will' myself back every time I close my eyes to sleep which makes slumber parties interesting! What's worse is even awake I feel, or should I say, remember death as **it** no doubt feels and remembers me; the one that got away! So, all the things I'm telling you (and all **its** faces), not all that nice, yet all too necessary. But first, I must tell you about the mean old snake who jump-started it all; then maybe you can understand the silent-conspiracy, the ghost warrior firefights, and the violent-awful rest.*

Most varmint, walk right up to your blind spot, but this one slithers in, wearing an Italian white sharkskin suit and matching alligator shoes. We watch him from the parlor window as he passes through our gate and into our yard. He slithers towards the walkway as easy as you please. Our guard dogs are currently at the vet's office with kennel cough; or they would enjoy a fancy chew toy. Somehow the overly bold fiend seems to know they are not home. He also cunningly realizes that Mom and Dad are away too. This is the one and only time of year when Mom and Dad disappear, for a couple's holiday. Maybe it's sappy, but it isn't my place to say nothing about it; no sir, not me. I appreciate parents not being around once in a while; add that the older-bossy kids are away and I'm just peachy. That leaves just us, the youngest three: me (Joseph,) Isabella and Isaiah.

But oh yeah, about that there snake. Hannah, our babysitter, directs us (Isabella, Isaiah and me), to the inner part of the house. She walks in the opposite direction, heading towards the front hall. I imagine her greeting the devil at our door. I follow quietly. When I settle, the visitor bares his fangs behind a pudgy smile. Even from a distance, he smells like baby powder. His stringy-spaghetti comb-over hair screams, "I'm 60 plus." I hide in the waiting room and watch through the side-window. The breeze flaps the curtain as I mouth and point to where the young ones--who are as stealthy as I-- should "go." Isabella and Isaiah silently obey, partly because I'm the oldest kid in the house right now.

I duck to one side of the window box and hunker down, quiet-like. I mastered Dad's combo gun-lock early. At age two (before they knew I had the gift), I saw the first combo number. At some point, Dad causally left the tumbler on the last digit. Finding the middle number was child's play. The double-barreled shotgun lay bare. I take it down and turn off the safety. It's already loaded. This old thing works really well. I did fire it once before, with the butt braced up against a tree. Truth be told, there is about as much gun butt as I have eleven-year olds' worth of shoulder. The shot gun's main use is to chase off river rats in the feed corn. It scatters off other thieves too. The salt load (rather than buckshot) is 'mighty effective.' Dad says that the war taught him killing is 'a mess, too easy and too often unnecessary.' That being said, neither this here feller, nor anyone else is going to hurt any of the Bookes family, EVER! I'm solid like Dad on that point. No matter what I must do, I'll use my 'will' to push harm away like I do with **it**.

Anyway, I peek out under the curtain behind the bay window and can see the snake. A round fingered hand swings his white handkerchief as a strike-out bat against the scoring mosquitoes. No doubt the bugs find a rare treat in his tender skin. I imagine there is no professional courtesy betwixt bloodsucking varmint. His slacks sway to his hand's motion. The snake clears his throat while standing on the first stair outside the mudroom.

My mouth is so dry that I feel my throat's heartbeat running for my teeth. I imagine that by now, Hannah must be facing him. I take a moment to angle the shotgun with the butt-handle firmly planted against the wall. It might not be a tree, but that wall is strong enough. Let's face it, there is very little I can do if that well-dressed varmint pushes past Hannah. But, if that old snake gets in here, he'll have to walk right past the doorway and me. I figure if I belly aim, I can send him hot footing it. Of course I plan to miss our babysitter. I have a good space for missing Hannah I reckon, but there's about to be some real nasty plaster damage.

"Well, Mrs. Bookes, I..." he says.

"Cause I'm a white woman, you know right off, I'm not Mrs. Bookes. So, -- what's your business?"

"Well, I'm Harlan Brummun from the State Bureau of Consumer Health & Safety: Field Office, here in Babylon County." He pauses to clear his throat. "On this day of Saturday, June 10, 1971, at 10:15 AM, I present these legal orders to residents of Rural B Extension." He pauses again to wipe his brow, then coughs into his handkerchief. As chunky as he is, I get the feeling he doesn't get outside the office very much. "And Mrs. Bookes or not, I need you to sign for this document served in accordance with New York State law."

"I see your timing involves parents, the oldest kids and all the pooches being off the premises," Hannah says. In the distance, just beyond the fence, I can make out Horacio-our farm worker crouching behind a bush and I'm hoping his machete is with him. Heart racing, breath pumping, like wild animal instinct, I feel a rush coming over me. I know **it** well and wait. But this here sneaky fat-fellow poses a different danger: the slow-poison kind. He's the creeper that attacks nestlings when the defender-protectors are away.

"Let me see that signed receipt paper," Hannah says.

"But of course, ma'am; I didn't catch your name."

"Didn't throw it," Hannah answers, drawing a deep spitting breath, but does not spray it in his face. Insulting enough I guess, the pencil-pushing types will not understand Hannah's *X marks the spot* signature. It's as good as a spit in the face anyhow.

"No matter," the suit says, as I slide back along the wall, ready to shoot. "You've been served with a cease-and-desist business operations order," says the snake. Next, I hear some scribbling sounds, and a far-from-sincere "thank you," followed by fading foot scuffs and a car heading to where only dark spirits are. Our screen door slams shut.

"Lord Almighty! Joseph. Come here!" Hannah calls out.

"Here I am," putting the safety on, and the gun away.

"I might have known," Hannah says rubbing her trembling freckled hand over my dark Buffalo brow and hair knots.

"Why?" I ask, looking at the thick envelope in her one hand as the other hand moves the butcher's knife (now visible for the first time), to her side apron.

"Because the Bookes family seems to stand up most when trouble is tallest," she sighs while looking at the package. "This is an evil packet I'm afraid. You know, I can hardly read," Hannah says with the first hint of fear in her voice.

I reach out and take the envelope, suddenly wishing I'd done more with Dad's shotgun.

CHAPTER 2
"CHILD OF ACTION"

"What are we going to do?" Hannah asks wide-eyed as the others come out of hiding. I look to the circle of children, then to our 25-year-old babysitter.

"Fight!" I blurt out, pulling the papers out of the package. Dad wouldn't let harm come to us or it. Neither will I!

The reading is all legal stuff alright. It takes nearly five minutes for Hannah to bring the kids (her son and daughter too) up to speed. Puzzling over the legalese, I realize it is a bit easier than Chinese—but not much.

"We got legal words," I say.

"Meaning what?" Hannah says continuing to twist her apron up and down like an ever-moving yo-yo in her hands.

"It's a *Stop Work Order* of some kind. We need a lawyer," I say to all gathered, as Horacio comes closer and is waved in. Isabella sings the Spanish music of our problem to him, I think; he grunts, then looks sheepish. Try as I might, I can't catch Mariachi the way my bird-brain little sister takes it in and tweets it out. I take in ole' fashion Yankee American just fine. Isabella's tweeting is something the English dictionary hasn't readied me for.

"We got words to fight with and we need a word fighter. That's a long-winded lawyer, for sure."

"We ain't got none," Isaiah manages without hardly a stutter.

"No, we don't," I mutter as I feel my stomach tighten.

"The ledger is in Mom and Dad's room!" Isabella chirps, with a hint of mischief none too honoring to parents. I know what she means. There are two things in the house not to be messed with: the ledger and the family Bible. The one is the worldly record of every dime we earn, loan, bank, or spend; the other is a spiritual reckoning of our names, births, deeds, & hopes. Betwixt the two, I'm pretty sure we can find an answer. Problem is Mom and Dad's room is locked. Going in there means getting skinned half alive; and skinning isn't pretty. Fact is, I only saw Luke the oldest, get it just once. It serves as a warning: kids don't nose around adult stuff…like shotguns for instance.

"What are you kids talking about?" Hannah says, "Can't we just call your parents at the Hotel?"

"That'd be 'swell' if they were there. Nearest I can come up with is that they're still on the road. Unless Dad's doing more than 100 MPH, they can't be reached for couple more hours…and well I think they'd say the same thing: lawyer."

"We can use the emergency list," Hannah offers.

"Police, fire department, pediatrician, veterinarian, auntie (who's with the girls), and the Hotel: you know those are all awash."

"What about the neighbors or the Traddish?" Hannah offers.

"Well, you'd be the neighbor we'd likely call; as for the Traddish Elders, they don't really have phones, or much use for modern conveniences."

"Oh, our church then?" She suggests.

I cup my chin.

"Maybe, call the church; the pastor or a deacon might know something." I say, as Hannah, trailed by her brood, speeds off to call.

"I'll go for the ledger, and I'll take the fault." I mumble. Their sighs almost say; "It's been nice knowing you." Dad and Mom will kill me! No need for **it** to do the job. I'll make it easy for him. Since I don't want Hannah to stop me, I won't tell her what

I'm doing. I just can't stand by and do nothing. There's nobody else here to fix this; so, it's my job! It's that simple. Now, all I have to do is figure out my last will and testament.

I guess my hand is right comfortable under my chin because I'm really trying to come up with a plan other than Dad's business ledger. All I can think of is that I have a big mouth and I ain't too careful about firing it off, usually until painfully too late, like now for instance.

When kids are bickering, Mom often says "a kind word turns away wrath." I haven't found that special truth to be helpful when I'm being Biblically corrected. By-the-way, there's been no rod spared on this child. Maybe, when this is all said and done, I'll only need a lawyer and a doctor, instead of the undertaker.

Mom and Dad's bedroom door is sealed. If the dogs weren't away, I don't think they'd have locked it, but that's the case. I study the door in silence.

CHAPTER 3
CALL TO ARMS

A puzzle work of door parts, screws and so forth greet Deacon Long and the older sons of the Bookes family as they arrive from church doings.

"Lord Almighty!" Luke toots as Peter folds his arms smiling. Paul (Peter's twin) just whistles in awe at the results of my screwdriver and pliers. The girls (Ruth, Naomi and Rebecca) arrive at about the same time--toting their throwing knives--with Auntie Clara who shares a similar sense of wonder.

"I ain't gonna' have nothing more to do with that door…ever again," Luke blurts out. I guess his last Christmas' spying would sour most of us to this here room. Mom and Dad use it as the early holiday vault before "Santa" officially places presents beneath the tree. Last Christmas, Luke got a mite curious and ended up with a lot of lumps that were as nice (I suppose) as coal. Anyhow, the girls make no sound which gives Hannah a chance at rapid fire explaining.

I'm naturally questioning which is part of this ever-spinning mind of mine. Besides, I figure I can't defend against something I don't know about. Like Dad says, "knowledge is power. Ignorance is weakness; and stupidity is death!" So, by the time the others arrive, I've already thumbed through the accounts payable, business binders and the ledger itself, numbers aplenty. Isaiah scans them. I read business files, then the family Bible notes. It is necessary, I keep telling myself. I see name after name of friends, family, and relations long gone, but never far from thought or prayer. The Bible is thicker than my waist; it's the oldest scripture in the house. The family Bible is worn even though the cover has been replaced three times, in my lifetime alone.

I'm careful not to move any of the dozens of papers and notes, especially those marked TAP - Tried and Proved. Each bookmark tells of adult leanings. After all, it is the ultimate Book of Bookes. I can't imagine a day going by without it being open, read, and used; that or one of the smaller scriptures. My tiny baptism Bible, which is still in my room, and new from last week, will get it's wearing from me. However, this big one is special. For one thing, it's the adult use (only) one... usually. For the other, it has all our names including the death certificates.

The one entry that stops me cold has my name on it! Reading it twice, I realize it says overdue and presumed lost, though it looks just like the other death certificates. I notice the wrong birth and "death" (I hope) dates. If not, I was/will die when I'm fifty. Unless my math is wrong, I was one years old when this Joseph Bookes, noted in the Bible as Godfather to Joseph child (so named) in honor of Uncle. Ok, I had an Uncle Joe, Dad's brother. I don't remember "Uncle." That's a problem since I remember almost everything. The other two certificates are for two children who rarely get talked about (Joshua and Jessica.)

Joshua and Jessica didn't survive too long after birth. Joshua, my twin, had no reason to die; at least I didn't wish him harm. I imagine Isabella's twin Jessica had no reason to go either. Old Dr. Siegel, before he retired some time ago, explained that twins compete for everything in the womb and that the stronger one sometimes overpowers the weaker. I know that's not the case. Old Siegel also believes that Dad's side of the family has a habit of twin births. At least Peter and Paul came out ok. I guess that's why my parents are so protective. I don't want to imagine the pain they -- or any parents--suffer after losing a child.

"Got Un-key-yell Sole Man Char Rails Row Man," Isaiah sputters pointing to the listing. To his credit, Isaiah solves this part of the puzzle. I frown, then read it.

"Solomon Charles Roman, ESQ, Solicitor/Attorney at Law…That's it!" I proclaim still thinking about the handwritten note with God-Uncle next to it.

"Just what are you preparing to do young Mr. Bookes," chimes in Deacon Long in his musically deep voice. I look to the gathering again.

"We can't reach Dad and Mom and this here letter…," I wave the snakeskin, "this legal stuff needs a legal reply which none of us is likely to know how to do. A draft, and a quick one, is needed. Weekend or no, we need this here solicitor-attorney fellow. And if none of you will…" Auntie Clara stops me cold with a firm (I got skinning pliers too Mr. Big Britches) glare.

"Well sir, looks like we're calling a lawyer." As usual, Josey, done thought it through clear and proper; "but, I is doin' the calling!" says Auntie Clara, while stomping her foot to the jingle of her dangling knives, making it all official: even Deacon Long says "Yes Ma' m," along with us kids.

I really hate being called Josey! Aunt Clara knows it, so I know she's mad, but not really. Not much later, I catch Aunt Clara's approving wink as she dials the lawyer's number. Now I'm not so sure how things run in other people's houses, but in this one there are two phones. The other general use phone is in the TV room. True, there is a phone jack in the kitchen, but sometimes Mom switches the unit over there; other than that, there it stays near the lightly dusty television. Just think, on a good day we get all four TV channels, until they sign off the air with the 'Star Spangled Banner' playing in the background.

One night, with Dad watching over me, I fall asleep. I rest better with my folks around. **It** doesn't seem to have as much power to claim me when they're around. Something about a warm hand on my chest helps keep me alive. I can concentrate well enough, but sometimes, I need them. I can't explain it. I just need them. Anyway, we (Dad and me) were watching cowboys and Indians.

One night, I made myself wake up in time to discover the National Broadcast Emergency Test signal, then white-noise and sign off. I have never really slept like regular people; catnaps are about all I need. For a bunch of reasons, I don't really trust sleep. It's Ok, I guess, when my parents watch over me; they do anyway. It's like they don't trust me to wake up. I can't say they're much wrong. It's not always easy to make myself wake up. The next day, Mom remarked that, "the TV enjoyed watching us."

Anyway, the TV stays off most of the time. Parents urge us kids to "go make play." Go read, write, draw, sing, dance, run, or just be out of sight for a while. If that ain't plain enough for you, Mom and Dad don't want us in the house, under foot, pestering them, and/or overeating. They don't starve us for food none, but breakfast, lunch, dinner (plus bread, cheese, fruit or mixed nuts here and there) is it; not counting the kitchen gardens with grapes, pears, apples (in season) growing everywhere. Otherwise, they don't want us within eye or ear shot until evening mealtime…unless there are chores, punishments, or issues. I usually end up with issues. I can't imagine why.

The other phone is in Mom and Dad's room so they can listen in! I've heard them pick up their receiver once or twice when I've been speaking to cousins who've called from Charleston. There is no hope of privacy in a place where "you" have every right to remain silent, present (instantly to obey) upon adult demand!

CHAPTER 4
LOCK, STOCK AND BARREL

I sense the hot salts in my throat and the sweet almond taste of blood. The night swells its dark claws around me like a coffin! I can feel **it** tightening my chest…I've fallen asleep!

"Wake up, Joseph. Joe! Me, get rid of **it**. Wake up now. Boy, get up remember NOW! Go away **it**. The law letter…the law letter," I tell myself. The trick still works. If I have a reason to wake up, I won't just fade away. A reason is all I need or …I startle upright.

Isaiah and Isabella curl up next to one another and I wake, not sure how I managed to sleep in the first place, let alone on my parent's bed. My heart jumps as I hear a strange voice, then notice the dwarf man sitting next to us. I could see no other of my kin, except the two sleeping beside me. I stand quietly, working out my options. I look around to see if Hannah or the shotgun are nearby. The stranger is holding my father's phone and looks me right in the face.

Solomon Charles Roman, ESQ, Solicitor/Attorney at Law, his name --I find out later. The middle-aged man in the beetle-brown suit points to a water jug. He's on the phone. I don't know why, but I hop out of bed and fill from the jug to his water glass. He views me sternly, touches the side of his nose –like a jolly old elf--and then presses speaker button on Dad's phone. Isaiah and Isabella do not stir at the sound. The mini office in the bedroom supports a desk, typewriter and a box of open files. Solomon's smile (somewhere between a Cheshire cat and a Florida alligator) is oddly comforting…since he's not hungry for me or mine—as far as I can tell. "Yes," he continues the (until then) one-sided talking.

"The original mild wines and gentle spirits were re-interpreted to medicinal elixir' and then re-phrased and 'interpreted' by the Babylon Chamber of Commerce through the Health Department as *medicine*."

"Solomon, that's mighty obfuscating, of Babylon," my father's voice booms from the speakerphone as the stranger (Solomon) waves me to silence.

"Kudos for the use of: 'obfuscating' We are speaking the same language." They chuckle again, and the sinister looking Solomon continues. "Yes, it is a very dark and thin use of the letter of the law; but as you know even vultures must eat." They both laugh again, as Solomon continues.

"When did you post your rebuttal and forestalling actions?" Dad asks.

"Well, Philip, it was hours ago, and Judge Tomlinson agreed with me," says the goat-like man seated at my father's desk."

"That hardly seems sensible, since the State (States in this case) took all their taxes and tariffs without much ado," Dad says.

"Yes, the Korean part of the contract is 'immaterial'...By the way, I'm surprised you didn't catch the 'mistake'."

"But that's what's peculiar about it. We've had the same (wording and) standing order for years. The same paperwork, baring the changes in international law you've been riding shot gun for us on," Dad sighs.

"Gentle spirits 'accidentally' translated to medicinal elixir and then to medicine. The words on paper haven't changed as much as the people interpreting them have. It's kind of a silly course for legal action, now" continues the beer-belly lawyer. Solomon gives off the smell of wet leather and the glow of Santa Clause's honorable North Pole librarian, retired.

"I'm glad you're there and could reach a judge," Dad says. "Oh, I agree! Although I don't think Judge Tomlinson was glad for my pushing into his tee-time, he's of the same legal mind. He even noted how odd it is that the documents you received were especially postdated and served on a weekend. With all the planning you've done for that little trip of yours, even Tomlinson --50 miles away-- knew when you'd be out of town. He says happy 30th anniversary and so forth. I suppose Tomlinson, at the county seat, doesn't talk to Judge Krishnan, in the township seat."

"Well, it's not a secret that I love my wife. I imagine you've already gotten the new translation and other paperwork done."

"Guilty as charged! I have a new translation…the Korean cook at Danbee's Restaurant and your delightful daughter Isabella…I hope you don't mind, but I used my power of attorney—that you haven't changed since the War, so I signed it. The courier service shall have it delivered by 9 a.m. on the first business day next week. I figured you wouldn't want any fuss near the Maryland docks. Imagine a poor State Trooper telling Bartholomew of all people; 'you can't deliver this load now.'" I hear my father's loud burst of laughter. I wince, Bartholomew?! Black Bart is a walking nightmare at 6'6" tall or more! I'll tell you more about him later.

"I don't imagine many people would care to go toe to toe with old Bart." Dad says, I can imagine his full toothy grin though.

"I wouldn't sir. From all accounts, Bartholomew has already offloaded the consignment to the cargo ship. By now, Bart is on his way home."

"That's great news. At least the vultures won't keep me from making my international delivery. It's a good thing we shipped a day earlier than expected; thanks to your gift, we averted a disaster."

"You're welcome. If you'd have stayed with the original plan, your shipment would be held on a dock somewhere. As it is, I was happy to 'gift' you with the upgraded hotel accommodation. I'm even happier to provide my legal services. But luck –or you'd say God's will--rather than clairvoyance plays a hand here. Just the same, the cargo freight-carrier should be well into international waters by now."

"This is the devil's own trickery. Them people!" Dad spits out, and I can tell he's most likely not smiling.

"Local government--them people (as you say) -- is devilment. As my people say, better the devil you know, than the one you don't.' They are predictable – to a degree. We can handle them, sir. The wine you sell either locally or internationally has nothing to do with practicing medicine or making pharmaceutical products without a license. I would have thought that *Mrs. Bookes' mid-wife, good wife & herbalist* status with the Traddish religious sect should not continue to be an issue, but evidently somebody…," Solomon says eyeing me as he clicks the speaker phone off and continues with a one-sided call.

"…is still using slings and arrows. Yes, I'll be here when you arrive. Hannah's gone home and your children are all here. Yes, it's been a long day. See you and Momma Rachel in a few hours."

Solomon hangs up and finishes off the glass of water, continuing to eye me.

"You have no questions young Mr. Bookes?" Solomon asks while lacing his fingers, pivoting the chair, and reclining in the seat.

"No," I say flatly.

17

"I'm surprised that my God-Nephew is so quiet. And not even curious as to whom I am?"

"Mr. Solomon and a lawyer," I say using my Sherlock Holmes thinking. The God-Nephew part I don't know, but makes no sense to seem less bright than I am.

"Good, I see you are well beyond concrete operations with respect to logical processes. Though, we were worrying about your lack of sleep," he says placing the glass down and continuing. "And yes, I'm your God-Uncle, Solomon," he says. I paused for a moment.

"But you're like Hannah. You're white?"

"How about becoming a little more discriminating? That means being able to make distinctions. I am a relatively pale-skinned Sephardic Jew. Which is a small tribe of Israel that lived 800 years in Spain. To answer your next question, I am part Spanish-Catholic with Arabian-Muslim influences. But all you need to know is that I have Jewish blood. And like you, I'm living in diaspora. So, what is your next question?

"Diaspora?"

"It means separated from home: Aklebulan…. Africa."

"Ok. What about God-Uncle," I mutter and process the other thought. "That's a lot to chew on." God-Uncle, my eyeball! He is more like a feral fire-fairy. How he keeps equal parts scowl and friendliness going, I couldn't tell you. "I don't know what that means," I admit.

"Well, for one thing it means that a proper Jewish gentleman has happily made the acquaintance of an upright black Southern family. As your father likes to say, we're related through Jesus' blood. And I imagine, from his way of thinking, that's how you had the good sense to find and call me. How exactly did you know how to do that?"

"I don't know. I suppose I got mad. My blood boils you know; especially when those stupid papers smelled of the law."

"Smelled of the law? Not everything in the legal word is nasty you know," Solomon says.

"I know. I suppose I saw the word "Uncle" on that card and thought you is kin and would light on our side a might quicker."

"I am kith and as good as kin. You're a might quicker is right son. I'm glad to see that the colicky baby I held not so long ago is growing into a proper young man. You are a little underweight however."

"Ok, I really don't have questions because I'm still mad and nothing really makes sense when all I want to do is kick a hole in something!"

"You are indeed your father's son."

"What do you mean?"

"Well, you're in 'angry but sin not' mode."

"That's in the New Testament!"

"Yes, not the part of the Bookes I enjoy most, but I have read it. Anyway, your emotions don't get the better of you because you know when to stop, seek guidance, and act firmly."

"Thank you," I say.

"Not at all, I wish more people would yield to their obvious limitations. You no doubt will piece this together tomorrow, but let's just say a few bad men don't like your father very much."

"I figured."

"Well, your father and I have been fighting these gentlemen, in their various guises, throughout the years."

"Why have we never met?"

"Did you ever need a lawyer before young Mr. Bookes?"

"I reckon not,"

"I reckon I am glad of that. I have sort of always been around. I wasn't supposed to formally meet you until later. There were many things to talk about then, but not so much now. It suffices to say, I am well pleased, particularly with your home schooling."

"Mom's a great teacher, but I need to go into public school to learn how to be more social."

"Yes, I've seen those State Test results. You're in the top 1% I believe."

"I suppose," I say looking towards the window.

"Your parents will be here soon enough, and things will work out fine."

I study the crease-lines beneath the lawyer's Ben Franklin style glasses. There is a hint of troublemaker about Solomon that suits me just fine.

"What does a God-Uncle do?" I ask him.

"Well, pretty much anything a Godfather does, but kind of loosely."

"Oh," I say understanding his answer and building an atomic bomb about the same. "Oh no, the lock!" I recall.

"What lock?"

"I busted the bedroom lock! I took it apart and now…"

"Young Mr. Bookes, I am not likely to advise impressionable youth in the art of breaking and entering, but if you would look, you'll see that the locking mechanism has been repaired, oiled, and set back into good working order. Now as to the disposition of your 'hide' when Mr. Bookes Sr., returns, perhaps you will need a better workman, carpenter, and advocate-- to explain yourself-- than mortal I."

CHAPTER 5
UP IN ARMS

"Who did this?" Dad growls smacking the law paper in his hand. My stomach tightens. From the kin line up, I step forward and find both of Dad's hands under my arms pits. "You think you's a man?" Dad bellows picking me up to his eye level. I look to how much of me ain't on the ground and how much of him is before me. Dad flexes his arms and up I go, to the clouds and back before he catches me. Both my legs go numb. He hasn't pitched me to the stars since I was two and the scary part is at 11, it seems to be just as easy for him. "What was you thinking?" Dad roars. "Well?"

"I was thinking, thinking of what you would have done." I mouth the words, not sure if my voice is coming out of my mouth or not, since I'm clearly still in orbit. I hear God-Uncle Solomon, clear his throat.

"Clearly, this boy is your son, sir." Solomon says as Dad sighs. I look to Mom who is all smiles and half asleep. Luke groans his disappointment; Dad might not execute leather strap judgment on my tender backside after all. "Joseph defended your house, Philip. He did well," Solomon continues. I try not to act scared, but I guess all 6 foot plus of Dad takes notice that the only big part of me is my eyes.

"Defended?" Dad mutters. "Broke into our room, rifled my files, and spied through my business records…all of them with his memory!"

"Phil," Mom says and gently places her hand on his cheek. Dad lowers me to ground level. "What Joseph did was proper and in line with how we raised him to think for himself. We can't punish him for being rational. That and who knows what those *townies* may have sprung, if Joe would have waited?" 'Townies' is Mom's polite way of saying: jerks,' she continues without a pause. "I think Joe deserves our thanks. After all, he saved the day."

Dad lowers his eyes to mine and kneels with a sunshine smile; he hugs me then rockets to his feet again, spinning me around and around. I feel part of last night's rushed dinner Hannah had prepared before nightfall, sloshing up into the back of my throat. When Dad puts me down, it's Mom's turn to twirl the rest of the guts out of me. I'm seriously thankful that God-Uncle Solomon doesn't take a turn too.

Saving the day or not, I didn't enjoy the fast-moving reward. Just the same, my tummy agrees it was better than being pitched skyward or skinned. Everyone is all smiles, except Luke of course. His frown speaks of a dark desire for me to get the same kind of holly stick correction he got for his Yuletide foolishness. The big difference is my actions are selfless. Luke's act was not. Anyway, I'm done with burglary and won't be trying that again. No Sir, not until the next time anyway. Momma's and Papa's spin cycle is making me really enjoy the solid ground I'm standing on – and not laying in!

"Well, that's settled," God-Uncle Solomon says.

"It's not the weekend I'd have preferred," Dad says bending slightly to shake hands with the lawyer.

"I dare say it isn't. But for the moment at least, the hounds are at bay," God-Uncle says as he smiles. "My usual bill, then?" he says.

"The usual," Dad replies. "We'll iron out the particulars tomorrow. It was a rough round trip ride. I think my bride and I would like to get some rest, but first breakfast." Dad says to a round of cheers. Mom all but races us into the house while Dad and Solomon stay in the yard. I'm not so sure what is going on there. I'm just glad no leather belt or hickory stick is being smacked against my gentle skin.

The golden pancakes, bacon, eggs, and home fries race to my well settling gut. No sign that they're spinning their way out. Dizzy as I was, I shovel down helping after helping. I recall all the names, dates, lines, and writing within Dad's multiple files, ledgers and papers. It's a large picture and none of it really makes sense, yet. But that's the second part of my trouble, I like to solve mysteries. I guess if I could get regular sleep, I wouldn't have so much time to think. But this legal problem, as Aunt Clara likes to say about puzzles, is a butte.

CHAPTER 6
MORE SNAKES IN THE DAYLIGHT

When even nature's birds and bees pause to listen to my brothers' music, it's not hard to live in their delight. Whenever either of the twins (Peter or Paul) perform and draw crowds, it is all but saintly. Their sound sweetens even the air we breathe. They are that good. I'm happily half asleep, teetering on the abyss then am revived by Paul's piano forte. The bliss and risk of drifting away to sleep and farther still somehow balance and I just float between worlds of enjoyment. I remain mindful of closing my eyes— but this time with a little less worry about **it**.

My older brothers have musical gifts which sweetly match the artistic skills of Rebecca, Ruth, and Naomi. We all have our special talents. Dad would not have bought Paul's expensive piano if the young man didn't faithfully honor God's gift to Him and us: the music. Likewise, Peter's singing is its own tonic. We love this week's family concert. Sometimes there are guests, though not this week, so far.

Hours of work and sweat are what we are supposed to do. However, rest and play are just as important. A dozen of our Mexican workers, as well as Horacio, sit in various parts of the yard drinking in the talent of my brothers; refined grape, pear or watermelon wines and spirits Dad creates for our livelihood. Mom bounds back and forth in her non-rocking chair while those little lines under her eyes go away and her beaming smile all but fire the hearts of the rest of us. Even Dad relaxes for a time though not for long. Peter and Paul play on to our delight as Dad excuses himself from the open side porch to greet unexpected visitors.

The shiny black limousine is out of place against the lithe music and natural backdrop. My snake alarm goes off. Standing at our gate is a man liked by a shrinking group and I'm sure, loved by even fewer. He seems very self-important. Dressed in tailored Navy sailor clothes, his fat body and round pale face give off comic book fakeness. He reminds me of a character with one dark and continuous eyebrow; and beneath his eyelids, two unlit coals glare a cold fire. His sight takes in everything; coveting everything, eating everything, wanting everything. This is Phineas, of the Sausage Sovereign Inc, Brummun millionaire, magnate and mogul.

He all but invites himself into our place but his hand is stopped by wisdom's warning. Our two silent Dobermans hold Mr. Brummun to stillness. They wait for blood, patiently. Even at a distance I can tell this greedy man is surprised that anyone or anything can dare say "no" to him. I can tell others shape Phineas into their own kind of Greek or Roman god. I imagine our Sausage Sovereign as Bacchus; after all, round is a shape too. Anyhow, Dad and the fat man fall into some words. But I can't tell what they're saying, though while chatting, Dad has the dogs relax and lay down; though they're still eagle eyed.

One at a time, my siblings and our hired help begin to sense some other drama unfolding. Peter and Paul call their own music break. After a time, we are in the yard. Still can't hear much of what Dad or Phineas are discussing. Brummun stays on one side of the fence just looking at Dad and the two killer dogs. All at once, Dad waves and Luke jogs to his side. My Papa points and for the first time in years, Dad leashes the dogs. Brummun waves at his driver, who's been standing to one side, and pulls open the car door. I move close enough to hear them, followed by most of my siblings.

"Give your brother Harlan my regards when you see him," Dad says. Phineas Brummun nods and smiles. From the car, a pale teen princess exits first. She refuses the chauffeur's hand and quickly bounds out of the car. She pulls her long sleeves down and adjusts her clothing before walking toward our gate. I notice her fancy shoes, her hat reminiscent of a Southern belle, and cloth umbrella. She almost immediately pops the umbrella open and floats an arm's length away from Mr. Brummun. Without looking at her, he continues yakking. He pushes a hand forward as if to invite the young lady into a hug. She silently holds her distance from the dangling arm until he retracts. Luke makes a sour face.

About then three other forms, tailored sailors like their round-figured father, appear from inside the vehicle. Three scrawny boys, not much younger than Luke, pile out. They are tall, pencil thin and fretful like a cat in a new house. Each boy sports the back-alley styling of 1950's film thugs: "rebels without a brain." Their 'coolness' is the store-bought and practiced kind. They are idiots trying to look tough, while trying not to get dirt on their threads. The stick figure triad gathers near the car, eventually lighting cigarettes and falling into their own mumbling.

In less than a minute the car door opens again and out bursts a kid near Isaiah's and Isabella's age. He doesn't pause. He's up, out and darting straight towards our gate. A moment's jumping up and down passes then Phineas nods, as Dad opens the gate.

"Nicholas Sweet, be careful!" is Phineas Brummun's only address. Nicholas rushes into the yard, ignoring the guard dogs and all but tackling Isabella with his hug. Nick succeeds in his next rushing embrace which topples an all giggling and laughing Isaiah. This kid, unlike his pack, is a joy-filled pup. Despite ourselves, we return his jovial greeting. Dad fully opens the gate to all. The three rebels and the driver stay near the car. But even the pale princess smiles though pauses at our dogs.

"This is Lily Sweet, my stepdaughter and older sister to Nicholas Sweet," Mr. Brummun says, in a general manner. Lily nods quickly as she pulls her sleeves down to cover a peppering of round, darkening scabs and pitted scars on her arms. Somehow, I feel the power of **it** nearby. Luke winces, looks away, then re-adjusts his grip on the leashes of otherwise motionless dogs. His smile turns toward the three stand-offish young men. Each of them puff feverishly on cigarettes as if they were candy going out of style.

"These are my three sons: Fendrick, Terrance, and Reginald Brummun," Mr. Brummun announces. "Is there some place we can talk?" he asks. Dad waves a hand toward the bunkhouse. My Papa opens the gate to this waddling-chunk of a tycoon. Dad, he, and Luke (dogs still harnessed), walk toward the worker's bunkhouse. Truth be said, I couldn't care less for his company. Young Nicholas, he's another matter. I have never seen a kid so naturally loving and lovable. The silly grin never leaves his, or our, face. The only thing is that he isn't much of a talker. Luckily summer sun and open grass need little talk or fun to just spring up all by itself.

Ms. Lily joins us, sort of. She laughs and smiles from the sideline. One of her arms is rigid and stays close to her side. She manages to hold the umbrella against her chest, careful to keep her sleeve to the wrist. Lily's sad eyes brighten as they follow Nick's merriment. But sour momentarily as they rest on her stepfather. She snaps her broad and gleaming eyes back to Nick having a grand time. Nick just invites us along his joy journey. His laughter makes us laugh aloud too, even Lily.

After some much needed lemonade, Nick points to the back area and Isaiah darts off with him toward the treadmill. Nick gets there first and stops directly in front of Old Dodges--Bart's draft horse that we borrow from time to time. The horse immediately stops and lowers its head. Without a beat, Nick is petting Old Dodge's head and offering magically appearing peppermints to a greedy steed. Nick examines the aging horse and the boy's face turns serious.

"He has a way with horses…any horse," Ms. Lily says. "I don't think this one is too healthy," she continues.

"He's just old. We don't work him too much, just to pump and cycle the cistern water," Ruth says. "Truth be told, we could use our generator, but Old Dodge is kind of a fixture."

"Oh," says Ms. Lily. Nick's kind hands trace the snout and jaw and satisfied of no harm I guess, he goes back to smiling.

"Children!" a man's voice roars. "Lily! Nicholas!" The two siblings look at each other, the horse and then toward their stepfather's voice. We walk while the round man hobble-steps toward his car. Phineas Brummun did not look back once.

"Children, we are leaving!" Mr. Brummun blasts. Nick waves and Lily throws a long wordless look toward Dad and the dogs and pauses on Luke for a moment. He stares back equally motionless.

The three pale rebel sons can hardly wait to get moving. They toss their lit cigarette butts onto the open road and climb into the car. All in all, comparing the Brummun brood, except for Nick and Lily, I begin to feel much better about having Luke-- block head that he is-- as an older brother.

"What was that all about Dad?" I ask as the Brummun limousine pulls away.

"Well son, that's about how a rich man acts when he gets refused," as he waves toward the road and the departing Brummun clan. "He just doesn't get it. He has heard 'no' a dozen times but keeps coming out here anyway." Dad sighs and wipes his brow.

"Not everything, and especially not this place, is for sale," Papa affirms.

"Oh," I say wondering if we'll ever see them (well sweet Nick really and maybe Lily) ever again.

CHAPTER 7
A THIN LINE BETWEEN

There was a milk loop dangling from the oak tree swinging empty in the summer breeze. If not for being so out of place, we may not have noticed the white rope. It was the tire tracks that first caught our attention. One of our Masthead poles had been vandalized. It looked like someone tried to cut one of them down. The fly- swarming pile at the base of the fanciest pole sure wasn't flowers. I guess the nasty pile is what the vandals think of the wood sculpture. Almost like the vandal's crappy calling card -- pardon the pun, is their threat of coming back to finish the job.

My sister Naomi took months of lovingly crafting to create the beautiful wooden forms. She'll be upset, but I know Naomi will fix this. Hopefully, she can hide or repair the damage with wood filler. These six huge poles are part of the large open mouth entrance to our place. Two support --between their wings-- the big overhead family name sign which hangs high above the turn off into our entry. Four of these totem poles tell a visual story and help frame the turn-around grassy area. These six Mastheads stand proudly against the side road forest, the clearing, and the dirt road to our place.

It also looks like someone tried to use a truck to run over one of the Mastheads and couldn't. I'm not surprised. Naomi's thick carvings are post-hole set about six feet with cement ground anchors. It's Isabella's sharp eyes that first locate and point out the swinging rope. Although we shouldn't have been playing this close to the road, Isabella --is also who—runs and gets Dad and Paul. Everyone else is occupied.

Some fool is sending my family a message. I stare in anger at the hangman's noose. The fancy rope speaks more of money than threat. It's marina boat rope. But Jack Ketch (the renowned executioner) himself couldn't have made a prouder noose. The image is frighteningly clear. It's also clear that no farmer around these parts has use for this fancy cord. Somebody wants us dead or gone. I guess **it** has daytime allies!

The perfect noose must have been hung last night. A local farm type would have used old rope. The new rope hangman's noose is up high in the tree and carefully made. It's just as exacting as its tree trunk anchor: a double loop snare knot. Whoever swung this thing made it sailor styled, ship-shape. This display takes lots of knot experience. Experience far above the kind I learned to tie from fishing with Sheriff Wits and Dad. The rope (new as it is) may have become quick garbage, except for my little sister's demand. Isabella begs Dad to cut a piece of the rope. Dad nods, slices and presents her a cotton-tail segment. Next the noose is passed to each of us. Each child rolls and stares at the dew wet rope. Paul's eyes glaze and a tear comes brimming but does not flow.

"Cowards," Dad says, as he takes hold of the rope. "Some people are just mighty low," he observes. A few cars slow down as they drive by. The lane just outside our farm is a county road. More often than not, it is empty, but a dozen or so cars seem to be traveling slowly by now. Three skinny motorcycle riders (some fancy dirt bikers) are stopped, puffing on cigarettes, and watching us. The red, yellow, and orange motorcycles --with matching color helmet-wearing riders, gleam in the distance. They watch.

Dad pays little attention to the three riders. He points to the weeds, then starts collecting small dry twigs. It isn't long until the five of us (Isabella, Isaiah, Paul, Dad, and me) are all gathering small bits of easy to burn wood, bits smaller than a thumb. Dad pauses to wipe his brow and considers the angle of the sun. He smiles and takes a paper napkin from his pocket. He tears the paper towel to tiny shreds. We gather around him as Dad tries the wind, tests its direction, and backs the shreds against roadside stones.

With sharp strokes Dad draws grated metal against a flint. Sparks shower shredded napkin bits until they smolder. In the center of the stone circle, Dad adds the shreds to the thirsty little fire which drinks them all; the hungry little blaze devours the twigs as part of its growing diet. Since the stone circle is near the mouth of the main roadway, slow moving motorists seem as quiet as the noose.

The process is slow and as exact as Isaiah's various counting. I can almost see my younger brother at his quiet pastime. He watches different parts of the tinder, staring sometimes at twigs and sometimes at napkin shreds. But always there are the spinning numbers and the flash of them in my younger brother's eyes. Isaiah doesn't talk much. His stuttering requires a loving ear to understand. His accounting of detail, however, is flawless. Isaiah's care at the count comes like Dad's care with the dancing flicker. Little by little, and banked amid the rocks, each twig folds into the yellow-red blaze, becoming its own part of the fire.

I can't help but think Dad could easily use lighter fluid and a match to fast track this fire. Instead, he takes his time, purpose-driven and slow: like it's part of a show; a show of strength and intent of which I can only imagine its origins. We add twigs, sticks, and small broken branches until the heat of the summer fire makes us step away. At this point, Dad nods and bundles the rope through its own noose and pitches it into the flame.

Without being asked, Paul begins singing the civil war *Battle Hymn* over the billowing smoke and crackling fire. Dad stares down the road. The song, the fire, and Dad's eagle eye seem

32

to become one. The clown-colored motorcyclists, one after the other, toss their cigarette butts, put on their helmets, and retreat as "His truth will carry on," bursts forth brilliantly. The song silences the birds, bees, and even the wind seems to take notice. Paul's voice is always soulful; now it majestically belts out a challenge of his own...our own. By the end, tears are rolling down my cheeks.

Dad stands and (for the first time today), I see his holstered firearm. "Lowly cowards," he says staring after the motorcycles as they speed away from view. "Well," he says over the traffic sounds and with his palm heel resting on his pistol, "we'll have to pay someone a special visit." Ending the fire is not as involved as beginning it. After a few minutes watching Dad nod to himself, out comes a shovel and he buries the smoldering embers in the dirt. Dad waters the buried fire from a rain barrel as I watch the steam and smoke. I shake my head.

In the station wagon, Dad piles us in and drives us back down to the house. He doesn't say a word. On the side porch he takes his pistol apart, cleans it, checks it, and puts it back together. Dad disappears into the house and returns without his firearm.

Within ten minutes, Mom and Ruth arrive together from some woodland chores. Dad greets them and whispers something to Mom. She smiles and nods. Mom tells Ruth something and the daughter juts off, returning with the other big girls. Dad nods, Mom points, and Rebecca, Naomi, and Ruth run to complete some tasks. Not long after, Dad makes all the little kids line up on the porch with him. He combs our hair, dusting off our clothing and so forth. Dad makes us get back into our road trip white van. We usually go on day trips in this oversized vehicle. The girls, and now the rest of the big boys, arrive. The girls and Mom load a couple of good smelling baskets into the rear of the car, and the rest of my kin pile into the van.

The drive takes us far into town and beyond. I watch the landscape change from weeds and saplings to fancy lawns and the iron gates of Babylon's rich folk. It isn't long until we are in front of a tall dark iron gate. I imagine the fire Dad's going to start here won't be a small one. Dad stops the van at the main gate. We all pile out and Mom takes a long ribbon from her purse.

"Children, wave to the security guard," Mom says.

"Where?" Luke asks.

"The man at the post box over there. See?" Mom points. We wave and smile, like it's Christmas. At first, he doesn't move but then picks up a field phone.

Ignoring the sentry, the girls go to work. They organize a beautiful bunch of flowers. I watch Mom and Dad tie a large yellow ribbon around an old oak tree nearest to the metal name plate with the Brummun crest on it. The girls arrange the flowers in a basket and leave it just under the ribbon. From seemingly nowhere a card/envelop, boldly labeled 'The Bookes Family' appears and is placed on the Valentine-like flowers. Nodding his approval, Dad loads us all back into our family vehicle, waves goodbye to the silent sentry and heads for home. For a good while, it is all silence as I stare at the backs of my parents' heads.

"Why'd we do that?" I ask. Mom touches Dad's shoulder. Dad clears his throat.

"As much as is within you, if at all possible, live peaceably with all men…Be not overcome with evil, but overcome evil with good," he says. All the way home, I think about the fattest Brummun snake and wonder if he really understands the kind of spiritual fight he's entering.

CHAPTER 8
NIGHT TERRORS

"I'm falling. Falling!" My heart is in my throat. Can't breathe! I'm crying and begging, pleading and clawing air. The rushing ground is my bulls' eye. I scream! I pitch to one side and…fall off my mattress smashing headlong onto the bedroom floor with a real scream, real pain and the real arms of Mom all around me. She holds me and coos me back from my wide-eyed 'night terrors,' as Dad calls them. I hate **it**. When I can't 'will' myself awake fast enough, **it** plays this cat and mouse game. How can I help myself or anyone else if I'm bullied in my sleep? Maybe the hangman's noose we found is getting to me, or maybe it's my old enemy: **it**.

Any way you slice it; I have a problem. Insomniac extraordinary! I don't really sleep all that much, which isn't the real problem. Guess I can get a lifetime of saving money on pillows, bedding and such. But it's when I do sleep that I get these dreams. It's because of **it**. The dreams are so real, so vivid. For my failed twin, Joshua, I'm thinking these dreams were deadly. I'm trapped, stabbed, hunted, eaten, buried, drowned; you name it. **It**, the dark siren, keeps calling me to where I don't want to go. Death has a taste of me through my twin's blood. **It** wants the other half of this unwilling meal.

Most of the time, I can focus myself away from dreams, but some bad ones still get through; then, I dream death in living color with a front row seat. **It** just won't leave me alone! I don't tell anyone about the dreams anymore. Somehow Mom still knows. The same way she knows how to touch my skull or tummy and make aches go away. She just knows.

I'm not completely sleepless; that would be a sure death sentence or a guaranteed place in the nut house. Luckily, I take short naps like old people do. It's easy for me to wake myself from them. Then things are fine. It's the longer periods that are a problem. Don't get me wrong, not all my dreams are doom and gloom. It's just that the bad ones are the most memorable. I don't tell young Dr. Siegel about the dreams either. Old Dr. Siegel knows the whole business. Young Dr. Siegel, who took over his father's practice, told my parents that all people need sleep but that the amount is, "specific to the individual." Well guess what; I'm REALLY specific!

It used to freak Mom and Dad out that I am awake most of the time. They've gotten more used to it. I'm not used to it. I hate this junk. Imagine that every time you really settle into a good night's sleep a bucket of ice water gets dumped all over you. How would you feel about closing your eyes? Sounds like fun. The need for sleep versus the sure knowledge of a sudden shock, don't balance one another out.

These night terrors unnerve me. I doubt my peace and find little rest. I don't know why I'm being punished, but it makes me mad; the angry (not crazy) kind and creative. I might not be able to enjoy a full rest, but while I'm awake, I really see things in ways others don't. Like a dogged detective, I end up questioning. Sometimes I scare myself at how I seem to processe ideas. It's like I just instantly know things. Generally speaking, I'm a good problem-solver, but I'm also like a computing machine with no off switch. My mind and will are also my weapons against **It**; and I'm winning…sort of.

CHAPTER 9

ITS TIME HAS COME

"It has been too long Joseph, too long indeed. But" he says with a pause "I think I have a solution for your '**it**' problem," continues Doctor John Roderick Siegel Sr., the Chief Research Officer, Executive Director and Chairperson of the fancy pants college; Reardon University of Science & Health Technologies (R.U.S.H.). in Rochester. Over the years, I told my old doctor almost everything, even the fears I had stopped telling my parents about. Not for secrecy, but something else. Behind Doc's wolf grey eyes is the hunter of wrongs which is what I need. He is bound by a love of life beyond my understanding to help me get rid of **it**. His hands first helped defend me from **it** and witnessed my first living breaths. I just understand that he's been on my side from minute one of my life. That's enough.

Earlier today, Mom, without discussion, drives me into the city to see Old Dr. Siegel in his new career. After my recent 'night terror' she has been all pills and poking and prodding. Now, I guess she wants an expert to pick through to the problem.

Mom treats my sleep problem like a disease. Dad treats it like an annoyance. My kin just think I'm weird. Anyway, Old Doc Siegel, you got to love this guy. His idea of retirement means go from being a country doctor to a big city-slicker super paid college brain/head guy; research medicine they call it. I mean he has always liked working with tough cases like mine, but retiring into a harder job. That's nuts!

"Do you remember what I told you last year…oh but of course you do, humor me." Doc says in his usual shot gun speech.

"Well, you said most folks who don't get much sleep sort of short circuit, and a bunch of negative mental and hormonal 'depletions' occur." I reply.

"Exactly so, but in your case, there is an aberration." He says.

"Aberr-a-tion? I've seen the word in print but never heard it pronounced before."

"Yes. Not surprising. Silent readers don't always have verbal samples. You aren't getting sick from sleep loss, though you're having some pretty wild dreams. I think my current sleep study will help. I have a good idea of what's going on with your 'it' situation."

"Dreams and death are my favorite combo… put me in the psycho-ward?"

"Not a chance. You're far from a basket case. Not every doctor gets a patient like you to document from birth. Can you still wake yourself up on a volitional basis?"

"Doc use regular words!"

"Quit pretending you don't know exactly what my 'big words mean," Doc chides. "We both know you're very smart."

"Yes. I'm my own encyclopedia but I'm practicing regular speak." I clear my throat and continue. "Not everybody wants to use a dictionary to keep up with a conversation, you know." I pause to look out the window and then back to Doc. "When I meet people, in public school for instance, I don't want any trouble or special attention. Being 11 and doing honors level high school work is plenty of 'attention' already."

"Oh, but you know the saying about putting a candle under a basket."

"Yes. Nor do people light a lamp and put it under a bowl. Instead, they put it on its stand, and it gives light to everyone in the house.' Matthew 15:5"

"Exactly! You, my young friend, shouldn't dull yourself. Ever!"

"Thanks Doc. I also shouldn't be too prideful because…"

"Pride comes before destruction, Proverbs 16:18" Doc interrupts.

"Exactly right! I might be smarter than some folk. It doesn't make me better than any of them. And I shouldn't rub my gift in their noses," I say.

"Gift? No, sir you have gifts and listening to your mother's wisdom is among them,"

"She wouldn't have it any other way!" I say and we both laugh. Mom's just outside in the connecting room. Part of every visit to Doc is a one-on-one session.

"Ok. I'm going to take you into another room with five other subjects. Your mother will join us there. We're going to run a special EKG electrocardiogram (we've never done one on you before) and if I'm right, I'll have a solution to your **it** problem that you may really like," old Doc says while rubbing his cold hands together. "Let's get started." We join Mom and walk a few doors down to a room containing five beds.

On one bed a patient is strapped into all kinds of wired craziness. His chart says he's a coma patient. Two others are old people snoring as we walk by. The fourth is a kid like me, but he stares into space, drooling. His chart says cranial-trauma victim. The fifth fellow is a genuine yogi – turban and all. He's sitting there, awake, I guess. I really couldn't tell since he wasn't talking, moving, or responding to his wire-bound situation. He has wires everywhere. His chart (which Doc encourages me to read) says the dude is an Eastern medicine teacher. Each of the five EKG set-ups and their respective wires lead into a fancy box.

"Joseph, that box is new. It's part of a microprocessor- a supercomputer. We're moving away from floors full of computers to just a few rooms. The school developed this technology for the space program, but we're discovering other more down-to-earth uses. Today, we're using it on you guys." Doc says. Mom nods. I just stare ahead at the place where I'm supposed to be sitting. It's not a bed, but a chair. "What do you want me to do?" I ask.

"Oh, sit in the chair and read this entire novel," Doc says pushing a sea-going pirate kind of book into my hands." How long will it take you?" he asks. I study the cover and read the back cover.

"It's only 200 pages, so about an hour," I tell him.

"Perfect. Your Mom will be in the next room, monitoring you as always." Doc says. Mom smiles and kisses my forehead.

"Enjoy your reading," she says.

"Yes, Mom," I say as she walks out through a door.

Doc gets to the business placing the cold round sticky EKG pads that sprout wires. It's a good thing I'm wearing shorts and a tee since the pads get glued all over my head, chest, arms and legs. I guess I look like a bunch of reeds dangling from a vase, though I can sit easily enough. It's not long until I'm chair-idled but bound headway into a sea adventure.

I don't think the other five motionless guests mind me enjoying a good read. I finish the tale as Benjamin Franklin's character thinks about honoring, the main character, Peace of God. But, instead of public glory, the hero returns home quietly with a simple blue ribbon as a gift and token of his unbelievable patriotism and self-sacrifice. He gives the ribbon to his daughter

Nancy, for her hair! I enjoyed the novel so much I barely gave the wild wires and clinical setting a thought.

"Finished!" I announce. Doc, who is no doubt watching me on the other side of the double mirror (presumably with Mom), quickly enters the room.

"Good. Good." He says "Let's get you out of these wires and Mummy wrap," he comments as he unwires me. "I'll have some instant data for you and if I'm right, Christmas comes a bit early for you," Doc says as Mom alcohol squabs the round sucker marks left from the stickers. "I'll be back in a minute or so, if you two could just remain here, it would be helpful."

"Okay," Mom and I say as Doc disappears and leaves us in the ward.

"I hope he can help us. He's always been such a good family doctor. I wasn't happy when he handed us over to his son," Mom says. "But I guess the young Dr. Siegel is just as caring and competent," she continues. Mom is holding me, stroking my head and from the reflection in the mirror I can tell she's worried.

"Young Doc is great. Old Doc is wise." I say as Mom nods and kisses the top of my head. Old Doc takes his time as the elderly couple's snoring, versus the motionlessness of the coma kid starts to get on my nerves. I hadn't heard them when I was reading, but I do now.

Doc returns with charts and smiles. "Let's go to my office."

CHAPTER 10
IT'S UP TO ME NOW

"That makes no sense!" I scream, smacking the chart paper.

"There it is in black and white," says Old Doc smiling.

"Am I a Mummy?"

"No. Your heart rate and vitals are lower than a master yogi's but not as flatlined as the coma victim." Old Doc says beaming, because I know he has more.

"My son has a lazy heart?" Mom asks.

"No, quite the reverse, Joseph has the most efficient metabolism (heart, lungs, and brain waves) I have ever seen. Thanks to the new technology we're able to see things I never could have 10 years ago. Moreover, these numbers suggest that Joseph was asleep while reading today."

"What!?!" Mom and I both exclaim.

"Young man, think of it in terms of some futuristic car. Every time your 'car' stops at a red light you turn the engine off, idle, and conserve fuel. When the traffic signal light changes you automatically turn the engine (your body) back on and move," he says. I stare wide-eyed. "Joseph," Doc continues, "You may be the first recorded human who has an atypical lucid sleep-walking condition. Your mind is fully active, fully aware and engaged while you sleep with your eyes open."

"Baloney, I remember every last word I read today," I say.

"Well, that's your other gift. But think about it. You get two hours of nighttime sleep, wake yourself on an internal command, and pretty much have total recall. Lucid sleepwalking and your bad dreams now make perfect sense. The dreams are a release valve or coping mechanism for your highly stimulated and optimally used mind. Maybe at some chemical level the body can't quite keep up with your gifted mind." Doc pauses. "Rachel," He says gently to my mother, "I need to say something clinical that may be uncomfortable for you parentally. Do you trust me to say it to the both of you?" Doc asks. Mom nods. "Okay then, Joseph, your birth incident --I'm sorry Mrs. Rachel and the loss of your twin--also make sense. You adjusted to the new environment outside of your mother and your twin just reverted to his fugue-like dream state, unable to redirect resources to cope with the stress of this world, literally. Even as a baby, you took an unprecedented command over your thoughts, actions, and physiological processes. With these numbers it's only logical. You're not an undead Mummy, grave walker, zombie or spook, Joseph, you're the opposite: you're living optimally. You, my young friend, can sleepwalk and cognitively function interchangeably. You only need two hours of bed sleep because you could be partially (if not naturally) asleep even right now. If that's the case, the nightmares are under your control too. If my theory is right, you're still thinking through problems when you're sleeping, and the answers (if not processed) come out in small parts as night terrors. If that's the case, you can literally think-dream them away!"

"I'm cured?" I ask.

"You were never sick," Doc Siegel says patting my shoulder.

CHAPTER 11
VISION OF THINGS TO COME

I might not die suddenly in my sleep, after all! It's hard getting use to the "sleepwalking and fully functioning thing." Were it not for church, I'd think I was some kind of sleepless monster. That sounds so much easier, but my brain works…too much it seems. Anyway, Old Doc Siegel from R.U.S.H. Rochester is right about the dreams. Without much effort, I can now turn them on and off. I can even make myself dream a complete trilogy and pick up where I left off the night before, if I want to. **It** is dead! Final and forever, free of terrors, unless some part of me wants **it**…No! Just the same, for a while, Mom is happy, because I am happy — and I gain some weight for the first time in a long time; but one thing I know about life; don't count on things staying the same.

All is well; Old Doc Siegel has me thinking about my dreams so much that I nearly miss out on the family doings. While I was sleeping ha, ha, Dad and Horacio suddenly disappeared. They are gone. They are on a sudden road trip; and that's why, for a while at least, the red truck is parked outside our gate. Bart, the truck's creepy 6 foot 6-inch-tall owner, moves about silently and nearly invisibly. When seen at all, Bart spreads (from the truck bed) wheelbarrow after wheelbarrow of ebony-soil to our side kitchen garden. Composting - one of the many things he does (I'm guessing) with roadkill. And then, like the animal forms that are soil now, he disappears: bubbles in the earth.

Days ago, there was that frantic midnight call I overheard, as Horacio roused from the bunk house and the marathon began; five days at noon now. Dad calls Mom every day before lunch. They talk for an hour. And then she shares--just a little-- of the information. Mom's report to us kids only takes minutes. I can't imagine what would be so important as to stop our business here and have Mom so tight-lipped. I really can't figure why 'he's' here at all; our workers' lodgings are now considered the bunk house of fear. Bart, all of him, is here, there, and nowhere. Try as I may, I can't dream Bart away.

Bart moves around our place with an ease all too ghostly. At least we won't have to worry about that old snake coming around here. We haven't heard too much lately about the nasty doings of Harlan and Phineas Brummun: but who knows. Since the flowers and yellow ribbon incident, I don't think they know how or what to do with us. What can you do to people who are nice to you when you've been undercover nasty to them? As it turns out, the Brummuns are better prepared (or more willing) to deal with the legal fight God-Uncle Solomon spearheads. So far, the Chamber of Commerce and Health Department people have stayed away from us. I imagine they'd plain runaway if Bart scowled at them. How a flesh and blood man can be here every day, but unseen is beyond me? Yet, I know down deep that he's watching over us; a good-bad spirit if you will. As much as it scares me to know he's here, not knowing exactly where he is, is the worst. All ghoulish-like, he prowls our property; the children are nervous, but our Dobermans Slim and Slash are joyous.

An occasional high pitch-whistle and the dogs are off to field or wherever the sound is coming from. It's enough to unsettle me. Our dogs are going puppy-loco at what I imagine to be the sound of Bart's throaty wailing. Maybe being a monster himself, he can speak dog and animal? The Dobermans only snarl at visitors, but this outsider is met with prancing Christmas folly. Part of me is a bit jealous. Sometimes I can get a bit of a romp out of the Dobermans, but this level of exuberance is unusual. Is there such a thing as 'dognip?' I must ask our herbalist.

Sage Mom seems unconcerned about anything, until noon each day. She answers the phone with a hushed, mild tone. I catch flashes of worry behind those all too knowing brown eyes. To make matters worse, she's sitting right by the blasted thing so nobody else can answer first! It's all a fellow and family can do to keep from going crazy. Each one of us has our own guesses.

The boys figure something horrible is happening with a friend's family elsewhere, and that Horacio is needed or somehow involved. The girls guess it's about Horacio's green card. I'm guessing it's something powerful foul if Bart is left in absentee charge of us. Mom can handle herself well. Bart is muscle. He, for an invisible guardian, isn't so bad, but even Luke doesn't venture out after hours these days. He stays right here with the rest of us, for now.

Luke has his own midnight marches and keeps his travels quiet, but not exactly secret. Luckily for him, tattling isn't my style. Just the same, he'll get his one day, I'm sure. His raw reign is not worthy of note, yet. Besides, long ago, I've found some of his watches, rings, bracelets, money, magazines, bullets, and other stashed treasure. As much as Luke's secrets interest me, they don't outweigh the dread of an invisible Bart.

Bart is out there, and Dad is away. Mom seems extra busy with her housework churning lavender oil into gel and soap, then blending candles to the humming of her favorite hymns. It's all a fellow can do not to burst with curiosity. I mean why don't they (the adults) just let us know what's going on? I mean really, if Horacio has scored a great deal on some generator, 100-gallon kegs, copper tubing or whatever, why the big mystery? Parents are just too secretive and worrisome by nature. Kids are smarter than adults give us credit for. Well, it's day nine; and I hear hammering, sawing, and the whine of a grinding machine. The sharp chill comes later as I'm by the kennel when the giant stops me and my heart.

"Joseph?" Bart says without looking away from the wire he is mending. "Give me those pliers." I swallow deep imagining how he's going to skin me and pickle my liver.

"Yes, sir." I manage to hand him the tool and glance up at the wet-white surgical mask flapping up and down with each breath through his plastic lower jaw. Well, at least he has that fake jaw strapped on. I'd hate to see the raw shape of his jawless mouth. Just the same, the cloth still seems like it's the only thing there.

"That'll do nicely," he says half-grunting and half coughing. I just stand there and don't move or respond. "You're getting mighty tall, boy." He says, handing the pliers back to me, without turning. "Seems like you're well fed too."

"Yes sir," I force out.

"Well, you've done everything any good scout could do to spot me, haven't you?"

"Scout?"

"Yes, those fellers who go ahead of the main body to spy out the land like Biblical Joshua and Caleb. You make a fair hunter, but your technique still needs work." For the first time, Bart turns and so does my stomach. Whatever is under the rest of the white mask, I'm thankful for not knowing. The part of his face that I can see, is a twist of scars and burn-healed flesh. "It would do you no good, if you were of a mind to find me or your dad. It is mighty hard, even for professionals," he says with less throatiness. "The military taught your dad and me real well son, really well. In the meantime, when he gets here, give your daddy this list of things I've patched, fixed, replaced, or mended." Bart kneels and presses a note into my tiny hand with his paw.

Above the windmill, the birds chirp and the bugs buzz around freely. I suddenly hear gravel popcorning on the road behind me. It takes a few seconds, before I turn to see Dad's truck, with three people in it, coming towards our gate. I turn back around to witness nothing but vapor where Bart stood. He's gone; dark like the silent night he came from.

I race to the front gate in time to see Horacio and a young man hauling out what seems to be a metal mess best suited for the red-hauler or a hippy museum. Horacio's narrow eyes widen. He nods his greeting; as does the Native American looking kid with him; and then back to their business.

"Joseph," Dad hollers.

"Yes Papa."

"This here is Matteo, a nephew of Horacio," Dad gestures to the stranger as I fully take in the monster bicycle form; it's a jumble-form of weld, rebar steel and woven wire.

Horacio's round worn face is the opposite to those of his nephew's warrior-like hawk nose and dark eyes.

Dad declares midst motion, "Matteo will be staying with us a while." I gawk again at the mixed-up masses of metal wire holding two perfect bike-tires. I sigh pressing Bart's note into Dad's hand.

Something needs to make sense around here, just maybe not today.

CHAPTER 12
TRAVELING MATT

A runaway! That's all Matteo is? And boy, his family is none too excited about his arrival. I mean come on! I'm disappointed too; at least he could have been a killer, bank robber or master spy. There's no excitement in him leaving everything behind just to travel. I figure it's bad when what I imagined is better than reality. But then again, which reality? I could be making all this stuff up in my head and lucid sleepwalking right now, if old Doc Siegel had anything to say about it. But Matteo? That boy turns out, isn't one to disappoint. He is unique. The weeks speed by with this Native American-looking kid straight off a 1955 nickel, absorbing English--more and more-- like his life depends on it.

"Hannah is a bruja!" Matteo mutters while folding the laundry. Mom and Dad give everybody jobs while here. Matteo falls under the watchful eye of Hannah who at 5 five foot 2 inches may as well pack a pistol. According to Dad and Mom, Hannah is in charge. That means us children have to listen to her, and so do our visiting foreign dignitaries. "Matteo...no like... witch girl." He continues grinning and mocking his own rich accent with a hammed-up version. Matteo's real English level is amazing. He's squeaking out Yankee American a whole lot better than I squawk Mariachi.

I let him know, "she's not that bad," but it's clear he really doesn't like her, or authority, and/or chores. Matteo is right at home with field work though. In fact, he could easily keep up with the doings of Horacio and my father (no easy job). But Matteo's just not good at the polite society kind of doings. He likes to sleep outside. He likes to work in the garage; Matteo is so handy he's actually teaching Luke a thing or two about engines. This impresses me on two levels; one, Luke can listen to an engine--any engine--and tell you what's wrong with it; and two, teaching Luke anything borders on the miraculous. Luke don't study nothing except cars, as far as I know.

"Hannah, is straight out of the devil's house!" Matteo says soft enough for me to hear. At that moment, Hannah turns an eye toward us. She's still in the kitchen. There is no way she can hear us, but she can definitely see us really well. My parents are off on some hush-hush errand, leaving Hannah in charge. I imagine Mom and Dad are away dealing with legal stuff.

"Hannah is so weird," Matteo says.

"Not really. She got here about the same way you did," I tell him.

"Really?" he asks.

"Really," Hannah says as she glares at both of us. We nearly jump out of our skin. I'd forgotten, she can ghost walk like Bart. "Really," she continues "and you may as well tell him the whole story, or I'm likely to cast a spell on you," she says staring at the top of Matteo's all too silent bowed head. "Go ahead," she says folding herself into the chair behind us.

"Matteo," I say, "here's how her runaway story goes..." The woman crying in mother's arms, a pistol shot and an irate Sheriff's Deputy all together announce the end of the family outing. Spray and steam rose from under the hood of the stranger's deer struck peace van. The rosy-rust sprinkles from the underside of the Woodstock yellow van have a Martian half-life all their own; the rust kept falling like red rain to the bare earth. The inside looked like layer upon layer of poorly hidden pain. Gnats or fruit-flies (I couldn't tell standing outside), seemed to be everywhere. Guess the stranger woman was going camping.

"This sounds like a good story," Matteo says, "especially the part about the bugs."

"I don't recall all those bugs," says Hannah.

"Well, let me finish telling it already!" And they both grow quiet...

Nothing else sprays or oozes from the van. But, the deer, a goodly sized buck by the look of him, was at one level all ooze and another --except the festering fleas-- not moving; the 1960's style van was built like a military tank. Good for the passengers inside, not so good for things getting hit outside, generally. Directly my father's pistol shot ends the deer's suffering. Luke, Peter and Paul --who Dad waved away from him-- found usefulness elsewhere checking out the woman's vehicle under the not too trusting eye of the lone Deputy. The officer then takes possession of my father's side arm and holsters his own service revolver. The deputy carefully noted everything Dad said, then the young constable (he had no grey hair or mustache) took Dad, cooperatively, to the rear seat of the Deputy Sheriff's patrol car.

During his radio call, the Deputy is a storm of words and gestures. Dad's smile gives no sign of fear against the events as the shrill cicada "...more bugs for you Matteo." In the distance, Danbee's Restaurant and the shop window are full of nosey customers getting an eye full of the Saturday morning 'Bookes family show.'

I recall Mom's grease collections for her side business (soap & lotion making) came from diners around here. She had good business at our roadside stand, the *Traddish Homestead* and local Flea Markets and such. Danbee gladly gave up the 20 or so gallons of his old-used cooking oil, rather than pay for the township's disposal fee. Dan Danbee, Robert Danbee's son, waves and goes back into his diner no doubt to call old man Danbee at the other location—about something or other. The Danbees are doing well and as Dad tells it, they've always done well by us.

No emergency vehicles were called, since the accident happened right in front of where the Deputy was taking his donut break; it must have caught his eagle eye. I saw his flashing lights a few seconds after Dad shot the suffering deer. The children, the crash victims, and us sort of half-heartedly milled around. There are four of them: a newborn baby, a boy about my age, and a girl looking to be a little younger than Isabella, standing around Mom and their mom. The boy seems to be the mosquitoes' favorite chew toy. He's scratching head and neck, something fierce; the girl too. I silently praise mother's homespun chrysanthemum buggy spray. Not one bug bite, yet.

"Get the toolbox," I heard Luke say as both his hands found my shoulders, stopping any hope of motion or not understanding his request. I'm not so sure if he just wanted to boss me around or keep Isaiah and me near and out of trouble. "Yes, yo' old brother is bossy," Matteo nods and goes silent again. …Isaiah gladly comes along to help this time. I reckon he didn't count on any tender concern from the elder boys and figured he was better off with me.

I had a perfect view of the whole crash. The woman's van tried to dodge the animal, but bulls-eyed the deer anyway. I guess it was dashing for its life from another threat and instead found the woman's dandelion flower-power van. When the accident happened near us, Mom screamed and smacked Dad's shoulder like a silent smack language that he read in her eyes in that second of contact. He pulled over and she was up and out in no time, running towards this woman crying/coughing—in the weeds-- on the side of the road.

The toolbox is the big one, and it would have been better for Peter or Paul to carry it. Good thing Isaiah grabbed the other part to muscle it out. On our way, I heard Mom humming as she rocked back and forth seated on the sidewalk with this stranger woman and the newborn baby cradled between them. "I was pretty much out of it, that day," says Hannah, as I find her hand on my back. "You going to be fine," Mom soothed. The white woman just sobbed, hack-coughs and scratches though I see not one mosquito near her head. Her children surround them along with most of the Bookes family: Ruth, Rebecca, Naomi, Isabella; the girls all take to cooing like lost pigeons about this tiny, pink-skinned baby dotted with red bumps. I could almost have sworn I saw a mite disappearing under the baby's pajamas. The big boys all gathered around the deer and the local peace officer.

"Joseph, when you get back, fetch me my herb pouch," Mom says as I scoot by. The tool kit requires both Isaiah's and my hands; the slight swinging from side to side is the only way I could move it.

"Yes, Momma," I say as I make my way to Luke. He, Peter and Paul study the engine and start patching the radiator's spraying leak.

"That's it. Nothing else seems to be too damaged," Luke states casually. "It should start up and go without too much trouble." Besides me, none of the boys look back towards the deputy's loud barking radio. Dad seems exceptionally calm against the red-faced officer.

Returning to Mom with her pouch, I found Hannah, (the woman's name), less confused. Mr. Danbee was standing there looking at the Deputy's car more than at the girls.

"You may as well come in for a spell," he offered. Mom smiled at the play on the word "spell," since she is no witch casting "spells."

"I can feel her pain," Hannah mutters "What? Oh, never mind," I say.

"In a minute Daniel, I just need to chat with her first."

"That's all well and good, just don't get yourself in trouble again for practicing magic-medicine," says Danbee. Mom and he exchange a grin. Hannah looks on quizzically.

"Hannah, don't worry, I'm a practicing mid-wife, good wife, and herbalist with some well-established root lore."

"That's not a doctor," Hannah says lightly fingering her scalp.

"Nope. Only in 1860 it was a bit better than most doctoring. Some locals hereabout come to me for "common-complaints," and I've been known to make a tea-tonic or two. I'm thinking I have something for that itch too," Mom says, and Hannah stops scratching, then looks down sharply.

"Meanwhile, Dan," Mom continues, "I think a slice of that Peach Pie-Ponderosa you're famous for will be about right," she pauses, "all the way around."

"I think we can make those arrangements but how about Mr. Bookes and our illustrious Deputy Thomas?"

"Well, let the men sort that out," she says, then looks to Isaiah and me. "You two fetch the boys, when they're done fiddling with that van. Ms. Hannah, don't you worry none. They take cars apart and put them back together again as weekend sport. They know what they're doing...with cars at least. You two young uns' get from under foot!"

Mom has the habit of not repeating herself (often) and I'm not likely to want to go changing her ways. I suppose we were crowding Mom and her new friend. Isaiah and I got the toolbox back to Luke. He started pushing and pulling and moving big black hoses and after a time the duct tape stopped the heated mist.

Dad sits quietly in the back of the deputy's car the entire time. As much as I and I'm sure the others want to go over there, we keep our distance, at first. Police can do a lot and to tell the truth, I'd rather they did nothing to me.

"Now I feel your pain. Police are too powerful," says Matteo as he gestures me to continue. Besides, Dad sat there humming and singing hymns. Isaiah and I found ourselves right next to the police car, humming and choiring with Dad. Deputy Thomas takes little notice of us, and Dad doesn't wave us away. By and by, the sheriff pulls up. He speaks to the Deputy, then lets Dad out of the patrol car. Next the sheriff returns Papa's firearm to him; and we, Isaiah and I, wrap ourselves around Papa's middle. His hands rest upon our heads, gently.

"Phillip," Sheriff Witts says to Dad, "I should make you Auxiliary Deputy Phillip."

"Dios no lo quiera," groans Matteo.

"Thanks for the rescue and compliment but being a shepherd to my own little flock is plenty of supervising for me!" Dad says and they both laugh. "Well Axel, I figure on helping the boy yonder, then getting us all to the diner," Dad says.

"That's a splendid idea. Just call in the report later today, so I can write it up. Meantime, I think I'll have a word or two with young Thomas." He coughs then wipes his mouth before continuing. "And I'll see you for my special 'wine' come September," Sheriff Axel Witts says smiling. The wine-syrup at the bottom of the 100 galloon wine barrels goes into a bootleg-style still, then Dad brews German liquor for Witts. And that was that.

"Good," both Matteo and Hannah say at the same time (about the Deputy's blues).

I follow Isaiah while Dad joins the big boys at the van. It is just about then, as Dad walks over, that a coldness (out of place for the summer day) iced my bones. Black Bart's red-hauler truck pulled up and came to a clanking pause. Deputy Thomas looked at Bart, then snapped back to watch Dad. Nobody really tries to mess with Bart. A fact of life around here; when Bart makes up his mind to do something, he gets few questions about it. Without a word, the man/half-sized beast has eyes on Dad. Dad tips his baseball cap. The two exchange a wordless conversation. Bart gets out of his truck and effortlessly tosses the dead deer onto his flat bed. Satisfied with the carcass, Bart gets back in, turns his wheel and drives away. My heart rejoices! His clear-plastic jaw gleams. I wouldn't want to be around when his jaw accidentally drops off. I watch Bart and his "catch" as he drives off. Most of the family is gathered by Hannah's truck.

"Really," grunts Matteo then crosses his arms.

"Well, there is more," I say, as Hannah strokes her sleepy baby's back…

CHAPTER 13
STRANGER BIRDS OF A FEATHER

"That's no story," Matteo scowls.

"Yeah, you're leaving out the best parts," Hannah comments, as her toddler makes gruff sounds in Hannah's lap.

"I ain't near finished you two, just listen…"

"Ok," what have you boys been doing?" Dad's voice snaps us out of our Bart fog.

"Dad?" Uh. Yeah…The van starts up like a dream. The lady had left her keys in the ignition. Nothing wrong with it, except the front grill is a little deer-bent. The radiator hose, the source of the spray-- was old and dry rotted. I replaced it with a piece we had in the toolbox. It should hold. Other than that, an oil change and this thing will run along another 100,000 miles," Luke said wiping his brow as Peter and Paul used loose wire to close the hood and put the last of the tools and trappings into the box.

We all end up at Danby's. Mom has silently taken command of Dad's wallet. Just the way of things, I guess. Meanwhile, Hannah, and her kids (the baby, Al and Greta) are way deep in hand to mouth with a cherry pie betwixt them. Hannah is too busy laughing… "you have such a wonderful laugh too," I say as she and Matteo smile… just to mess with them and I reckon they had the right notion.

Hannah gets herself together long enough to wipe her children's faces. I noticed that her fingertips look black and rough. I guess I was staring, and she moved her hands away, scratching her scalp as her children did the same. It was about then that I saw things moving like a small crawling cloud avoiding finger touch. I had never seen anything like them before

"Poor children have bug bites," Matteo says as Hannah's other hand rests on his shoulder and his arm loops her middle… Anyway, we all had pie and burgers. Through the open kitchen door, Danby is a whirlwind of cookery. I couldn't tell how folk make five different meals in the time it would take Mom to make one. I hate to think he was a better cook. I'm certainly not going to bring that subject up. Luke's error long ago was plenty for me to remember. If Mom makes it, say it's great; if it isn't awesome…lie. "Your mother is a great cook!" Blurt out Hannah and Matteo at the same time again. This time they look at each other and laugh.

Dad finishes his official business and joins us. Dessert first is a great idea and the meal that followed was wonderful too. Feedings all done, it's almost like a silent set of instructions get us all heading back home. Luke and Paul take Hannah's van, while the rest of us pile into the big white one. It isn't long until we're looking at the long rough unpaved stretch of road where Naomi's tree-like sculptures greet us. The detailed Mastheads (as big as Totem pole looking things) reach skyward. Some things you cannot make up, even in your wildest dreams. Naomi's carved story tells of angels which I haven't quite figured out yet. I stare every time I pause to look. Naomi is a gifted sculptor. Over the entry road to our place—between angels' wings-- is the Bookes Family Vineyard sign. The strength of all three men (Dad, Horacio and Bart) with block and tackle, was needed to put the wooden angels and placard in place. The artistry is so good that I can almost taste the carved grapes and worry about the violence I see in the angel's eyes. The carved bottles so real looking I swear they're all ready to pour wine toward the sun.

"All of Naomi's art is really pretty. It sells good with the soap." Matteo says.

"Yes, it does, mind if I keep the story going?"

"Go ahead."

We pull into the yard and Luke goes zooming past us toward the water mill. He slams on the brakes, falls out of the van, then does a weird kind of striptease. Running, stumbling, hopping, and howling, Luke literally sprinted out of his clothes on his way into the river. Everyone laughed except Hannah, who seemed like a soul lost in shame. Her tears began again.

"No reason to be ashamed. I had all kinds of bug bites and bruises before the Bookes brought me here," Matteo says in the softest voice I've ever heard from that hard cut Native American jaw. Hannah's touch seems to lighten as her smile broadens.

"They've debugged us both" she says…

"Phil, see to Luke. Paul seems fine, as far as I can tell," Mom said again holding Hannah who tries to push her away.

"Don't touch me! I'll get you infested too," Hannah says between sobs as Mom holds her closer.

"Not likely. Chrysanthemum oil does a good job on many an "infesting;" too bad Luke didn't put any on when everyone else did. He wanted to use his store-bought spray and not smell flowery, so we let him. Oh well. Meanwhile, I got something that'll fix you, yours, and that van of yours. Just you wait and see." Mom says as Hannah looks up. For the first time I can see how young she is and how old her eyes seem.

Through tears Mom hears that Hannah is from the coal mines of Donora. As I listen and follow Mom from vehicle to side-porch, Hannah tells of her escape. She had packed up everything she owned along with her children a few nights ago.

"I just started driving away from HIM." Hannah said sobbing, then pausing to half-heartedly soothe her baby.

"I escaped from bad people too!" says Matteo shuddering ever so slightly while moving closer to Hannah. Matteo rolls down his sleeve to show several small round burn marks. Hannah touches his old scars then pulls her shirt down to her collar bone showing similar ring marks.

"Cigarette burns?" She asks Matteo.

"Cigarettes burns," whispers Matteo. They do not laugh at their mirrored responses this time. Each seems lost in a moment of deep thought. Hannah nods as her baby squeals then claps her hands together.

The older children (scratching more openly) seem less upset than their mom. As I look about, I notice Luke helping himself to the Chrysanthemum oils. I guess the store-bought stuff wasn't that good after all. Dad moved our van next to Hannah's then did a strange thing. He put a tent up around both vehicles, moved the liquor still into the tent and fired it up. He put the open copper-coils directly into Hannah's open van windows. He's steaming both cars?

"You get back to your mom," Dad says as he seals the flaps of the tent. One at a time, Dad takes Hannah's children into the back-up tank. Well really it is just a swimming pool, but Dad made it into a drinking supply by using a double sand filter and a charcoal filter. Right now, it's a dunking tank. Hannah is eased by Mom and doesn't complain. In fact, Mom walks her over to the hot tub, flicks off her shoes and lady, mom, and baby get right in.

"Run and get the lavender soap," Mom yells. Flying feet boost me in and out of the house with the homemade soap Mom usually reserves for family and close friends.

"I still have my soap," Matteo mutters almost as if he's thinking rather than saying.

"Thank you, Joseph. Now take some soap to your dad."

"Yes, Momma," and I'm off again. Isaiah is a faithful shadow carrying fragrant soap wrapped in brown paper in his own hand. Between fussing and peeling off layers of clothing, it seems like folk are getting a real wash down.

"Chrysanthemum oil!" Mom yells and Isaiah, Paul and I lug out four-gallon jugs.

"Towels!" Dad decrees and the family is a flurry of activity. We'd never bathed somebody else's family before and truth be said, it was kind of exciting. The late summer breezes were still plenty warm enough to support the outdoor cleaning. Protest as she might, Hannah really had no choice in the matter. Ruth, Naomi and Rebecca changed into their swimwear and brought out wine, bread, and cheese for Mom and guest. It is a little bit like the seasonal wine tasting bonfire events, though somehow nicer.

I knew we were not supposed to dirty-up the hot tub with oils, but it seems like the rule didn't apply that day. Water Reservoir # 3 could handle river water and make it drinkable, so I figured a little soap had no hope of poisoning us. From crying to gently floating, her laughing baby echoed the joy of all. Mom opens her pouch, yet somehow, it's not wet. She pours out a pinch then adds a little water to make a paste. She then rubs the back of the lady's neck. By evening, everyone had swum, or been in the hot tub, or river (in Luke's case), or the rough-built hothouse sauna (for Dad).

Even the woman's hacking cough settled to a wheeze followed by regular breathing. Hannah's eyes filled with a different kind of tears. Mom smiled.

"I ain't got nothing to give you," Hannah said.

"We don't charge a fee for doing God's work," Mom said.

"Oh," says Hannah out of nowhere, "I wish I could get the baby baptized!"

"You mean get the baby christened?" Mom advises.

"Yah, christened," Hannah echoes.

"I think we can do something about that," Mom tells Hannah.

True to her word, Mom summons Dad. She explains something then Dad nods and is away to the house. He comes back dressed in khakis and carrying a Bible.

"We got some christening to do," says Dad.

Dripping wet, Mom stands next to Hannah. Dad smiles. Within a few minutes we are set to do the dedication ceremony.

"Who offers this child in the hope of knowing and learning of our Lord?" Dad says as Mom nudges Hannah.

"I do," she says.

"The name of the child please,"

"Catherine Jada Rivers," Hannah says as Dad continues. He takes the child in a towel, drips some clean water upon her, says a bunch of stuff, then turns to us all. Without noticing, our seasonal field hands are at this spot, standing with us.

"Who will stand as Godfather for this babe, help her read the Bible and follow the ways of our Lord?"

"I will," I utter without a shake or tremble. Mom cups her hands, and all eyes are on me.

"Well, young Mr. Bookes, I'll hold you to it sir." Dad says as I step forward and press little giggling Catherine in my arms. "Now," Dad continues, "who else here will help guide, support and teach this baby?" Everyone said, "I will." And I suddenly felt 10 feet tall.

"Gathered friends, I present Catherine-Jada Rivers. I ask you to pray for her guidance, pray with her in the future and about her growth in the name of our Lord and Savior …and the body assembled said:"

"Amen!"

Echoes erupt as a tiny white Bible is presented to laughing and crying Hannah-holding her baby. That night, (and for a week), Hannah and all her kids slept itch-free in a real bed. Dad made a few calls and found her a job. Hannah now had every hope of her family doing much better. They would no longer be wandering the backroads alone, afraid of being attacked by crazed deer, while being eaten alive by mosquitos and bedbugs.

And that's how Hannah joined our family Matteo" Who responds with a simple "comprende."

"That about sums it up," Hannah says roughing Matteo's dark hair. "Now back to work, the both of you!"

"Yes, ma'am," says Matteo, but hugs Hannah clear off her feet as she giggles at the release. Matteo never muttered another word about the evil "bruja."

CHAPTER 14
AN EVENING WITHOUT

"Remember, you have a temporary baby-sitter tomorrow," Mom says. "Hannah and her children still have the flu; so, she won't be available for a while. Our church says Mrs. Pyle is a great sitter! Y'all just need to behave."

"Yes, Mama," the three of us (Isaiah, Isabella and I) echo.

It was the first day that week that Mom wasn't checking our temperatures, giving us vitamins, wiping our noses, or fidgeting over us. I got extra attention because of all the sleep studies at Reardon University of Science & Health Technologies (R.U.S.H.) and Old Doc Siegel—in his new job—insisted upon it. Mom is going along with it, though Dad couldn't care less.

Old Doc wants me to try something called "facilitated dreaming." Sort of like homework in your sleep. It's all weird; but hey, I'm no longer being stalked by Death while unconscious. I'll do whatever Old Doc wants. I owe him that much for my peace of mind. I guess sleepwalking with my brain on is scientifically interesting! I'm not trying to make sense of it. I'm alive and healthy! Don't care about the particulars too much. But, knowing what's going on in my body, head and life, is too cool. Not knowing could have killed me!

Anyway, Dad simply forks down more food. He makes little secret of his dislike of peas or of Mom's fussing about.

"Why?" I mumble, pretending to have forgotten about the long re-scheduled weekend plans. The original anniversary plan got busted up by the underhanded doings of the Brummun sausage clan. Giving the white devil his due, Dad manages to get back most of the anniversary deposits. He rolled them over into more local plans for his bride. Dad looks up to answer, I guess.

But Ruth replies before Dad can: "They always spend the day in town, remember. Every anniversary, they spend the day walking, talking, and laughing like on them French stories when young lovers go off to a romantic Inn and..."

"Well thank you, young lady! That's enough explaining!" Dad just grunts. All the girls but one giggle. Isabella scowls. Mom covers her grinning mouth. "Rachel," Dad continues, "wife of mine, please stop encouraging your daughters to read romance novels!" The youngest girl, Isabella, is still not amused. Dad swallows some peas and clears his throat. "We just going out is all...we'll be back soon enough. It's a blessing that the place can do without us for a day."

Isaiah sighs: Isabella rolls her eyes. I sit as still as I can.

"You other children make your new plans firm?" Dad asks.

"Sure did, sir" Luke spouts, "we going camping with the school's summer nature club. You've already signed the permission slips. Too bad the 'little babies' can't come along," Luke eyes Isaiah, Isabella and I. All the big boys smirk but one. Peter's upper body jerks as Luke straightens smartly from a well-placed kick. Luke scoots his chair out of shin range. It's not nice being called a 'baby.' I'm obliged to Pete; he understands the pains of us little people.

"We'll be fine," Paul says playfully cuffing Luke on his shoulder.

"Boys!" Mom corrects.

"Sorry Mom," Paul says and turns to Papa "Dad, it's a two-day summer science camp near Lake Ontario. You remember we couldn't go last year because of Isaiah's accident." As Paul says this, Luke scowls. Isaiah is a pretty good actor, but we couldn't pull that one off again.

"You just make sure to give me the emergency contact numbers," says Dad while meshing a mouth full of carrots. "Here's the number for where Ma and me will be. It's also stuck on the ice box," Dad continues while handing Luke a piece of white paper.

"We can guess what number you two will be up to," Ruth retorts. The big girls laugh outright, and Mom puts her napkin up to her face to cover her giggle. Dad wipes his mouth.

"Tarnation," Dad mutters, with a vegetable filled grin. Isaiah, Isabella and I just sit there quietly.

"Auntie Clara!" Ruth blurts out. "I forgot to call Auntie about our other arrangements."

"Other arrangements?" Dad asks.

"Oh, nothing Dad. Just more details about the knife throwing tourney. May I be excused?" The napkin is down, she's up, out, and all the girls but one –Isabella-- are at the living room phone. Dad smiles, swallows and shakes his head. The smile lands on Mom and she returns it with a long silent google-eye.

"We plan," Luke blurts out, moving his chair back to the table, "to go hiking and do rock-climbing stuff too."

"Geology," I mutter.

"What was that, Joseph?" Luke asks, lowering his sights on me.

"You're looking at igneous rocks," I'm preparing my aim-filled trap for him.

"Rocks ain't stupid. They can't be ignorant, " Luke falls for it! I pause, nod once, then smile at Isaiah, who silently urges me on. I fire back.

"Well Luke, maybe if you'd read your science book instead of hiding it, you'd know the difference between igneous and ignorant...ignoramus!" Nobody laughs.

"Young Mr. Bookes, " Dad bellows." We appreciate that fine vocabulary lesson you provided; now, what am I going to tell you?" Dad asks as I clear my throat.

"That...that I should go to my room with no dessert," I venture. Dad cups his chin with one hand stroking a side burn with his index finger. His eyes flash to Mom and then back to me.

"Another thing young man, you don't insult kin like that." Dad excuses me from the table but not his care.

I know Isaiah's eyes praise and Isabella's grin warms my cause, but best of all I hear Dad call for Luke to bring his science book to the table.

I take the dictionary with me, shut my bedroom door and face a chair toward the wall. I copy silently--improving my handwriting--until bedtime. I'm permitted bathroom breaks and that's all. I know the drill. Dad needs not check on me. Isaiah comes in much later, undresses and crumples into bed. It's all set; the boys go camping; the girls are likely planning an Annie Oakley Society visit with Auntie Clara. Mom and Dad go wandering; the 'babies' will stay home like pigs in a cold wet blanket.

Even for me, it is a fitful night's sleep. The morning chores are rushed, and breakfast is gobbled to the sound of girls squealing. As it turns out, Auntie Clara is taking them to the Annie Oakley Society Woman's workshop. Auntie and my sisters are all defending their titles and championship status in the Regional Knife throwing trial...again.

"I'm...me... going to that moon," Isaiah pipes up, " and mine cheese..." he says as Mom interrupts.

"That's precious," Mom says turning her ear. Isaiah shuts down and goes outside to the yard, I suppose.

"Girls," Mom says, "you need to be just as focused this year. Ruth and Naomi, you both made the State marksmanship finals last year."

"If I make State again then Dad will be fussing," Ruth says smiling full bright. Mom laughs outright and shakes her head.

"I'm cutting back on your TV time! You girls learn too many bad things," Mom says grinning.

"Not half as much as..." Ruth stops and all attention is on me. "Don't you want to go outside and play or something, Joseph?" Ruth asks?

"Not really," I answer.

"Out you go, the sun's shining. Go make play!" Mom points to the door.

Dad is too busy to even tell me to go play.

Luke is doing something in the side yard to that nasty old car of his. He doesn't have a license yet, but Dad makes sure he has a car first. The logic is pretty simple: Dad is putting full responsibility on Luke early on. If Luke really wants the car, he must learn everything in the mechanics' repair and such…formally and to Dad's standards. Luckily, Luke is mechanically minded. Dad is making Luke accountable. This plan has two merits: The one is if Luke gets stuck or breaks down somewhere, he could get himself out of it. The other is he'd have to earn the right to own a car. The family wisdom is such that if you sweat to earn a thing, you'll take great care of it. Dad is big on making us earn and/or learn our own way.

"Go away!" Luke snaps at me without much ado.

"Wasn't stopping here no way," I say as he frowns and goes back to his engine work. I figure he learned a lot about geology or humility last night. Dad buys copies of Luke's school books. More of Dad's learn, earn and burn philosophy, I reckon. I'm glad Mom is still home-schooling me. Anyway, I wonder where Isaiah is.

"Paul, give me the socket wrench," Luke commands. "We need to hurry, get showered, then walk to the bus stop."

"I'm hurrying," says Paul as he tosses the wrench. Peter looks on without a word.

I find Isaiah and Isabella at the front gate. My baby brother is raking a stick back and forth across the metal fencing. He's sniffling while looking down the road. I stand with them and stare too.

After a minute or two, Isaiah puts one hand on Isabella's shoulder. He then points with his stick as the baby-sitter's car comes into sight.

"Now," Mom reminds us from a distance, "mind your manners."

"Yes Mama," all three of us drone.

"And do as the sitter says. Don't look all sad like that. The sitter is plenty fun and..." Mom says as Dad interrupts her.

"...And you're staying this year, with no fuss. Hear me?" Dad asserts.

"Yes, Papa," we hum.

"I don't want to hear about no 'faked' accidents this year." Dad continues. "You understand?"

"Yes Papa," we buzz.

Soon the older boys march out to town like soldiers. Auntie comes for the older girls. Mom and Dad are the last family members to leave. They give the little old lady a few extra instructions before driving away. Moments after, the family leaves us to the care of the smelly old woman, Mrs. Pyle. She takes a small whiskey bottle and a drinking glass from her knitting bag. Thirty minutes later, she's sitting and snoring. After tying her to the chair, we smear her face with peanut butter and anything else we can find. Still snoring happily, she doesn't even stir.

It isn't until much later that Isaiah and I figure out Isabella must have made that horrible phone call.

CHAPTER 15
LITTLE SNAKE

Dad unties, comforts and pays the terrified baby-sitter. After Dad's call, Mrs. Pyle's friend quickly arrives in the same car he dropped her off in to take her away. The mustard, peanut butter, shredded newspaper, and pillow feathers, which are stuck on her face make a lasting impression, I'm sure.

"I'm taking Isabella out of this...this mess!" Mom announces as she kisses Dad on the cheek. He grunts. Mom snatches Isabella up. My baby sister buries her face into Mom's shoulder. Just before Mom disappears with a 'tearful' Isabella, I think I see 'the baby' [the architect of our destruction] looking back at us, snarling with her tiny pink tongue stuck out.

Isaiah and I discover that there's a 'younger' fork-tongued snake in Babylon. One secret phone call to Mom and Dad's restaurant is all Isabella does to cheat us of our victory and set us on the road towards disaster. Isabella not only tricks us; she ruins our parents' replacement anniversary as well. Earlier, Dad changed the old reservations—from their first ruin of an evening-- to a more local spot. But sadly, this evening ends in the same way: with a cancel, drama and a rush home. The only difference is the source.

The snake, courtesy of Isabella's phone call, my parents rush home to save the hog-tied baby-sitter, dismiss the crone, and get the bad guys [Isaiah and me], while rescuing their 'little angel' Isabella from the bad boys. Isabella --for the record-- is the one who found the rope for the sitter-tying! Why if her own venom ever does back flow, Isabella could be one fine mass murderer (or politician,) I just know it! There is no way to resist Dad.

First, Dad studies the room and disaster we've made of it. Then, he looks us up and down. Isaiah, my baby brother and I look to each other helplessly. Unfair as it is, the older boys and girls have a second long weekend too. Even Matteo is out with Horacio at Bart's farm. There is no help and no escape. Dad points: we sit.

Leaving us waiting, Dad steps out of the room and returns with the broom, dustpan and various other things. Neither of us move. Dad is still too old to be treated like a kitten. It isn't the fun fisherman Dad before us. It is the full-on-man of the house. It's painfully clear that there is no relief to come from his correction plan. He gestures us from the couch and gives us the cleaning gear. I recall my second thoughts about Isabella's silly dare. Why did that smelly old sitter have to fall asleep--and snore-- in the first place?

"Clean" is the single and only word Dad says during the entire first half-hour. When we stand swaying like saplings in the breeze of a forest fire before him, Dad checks the room, moves the couch, shakes his head, and points. Another half-hour, according to the grandfather clock, we again think the job is done. Dad's finger shows us otherwise.

Dad shakes his head and points to stains on the wall. He doesn't openly yell. Instead, quietly, he waits and watches. Isaiah's tears come and go like flash summer rains. Here and gone in barely enough time to prepare for them. With his help I got a bucket, water, towels, and soap. I hate cleaning the chocolate pudding off the ceiling fan, but Father easily lifts me to the splatters. My trembling lips go unnoticed as I consider Dad's crushing jaws, his beam-like arms and his huge powerful paws. At one point, Isaiah wins his plea for a bathroom break that seems all too short even to me. He returns only a little better.

Dad points to the TV and we clean the screen, back, behind, under, and sides. Dad points to the corners and we clear, pick and wash. He points to the carpet, and we vacuum, brush and scour. I even scrub an old stain out of its strong hold. Every time we go before him, there is no pity given. We did the same task again and again until it was done to his liking. He likes it a little.

I catch Mom spying on us before she hides behind a door crack. There will be no rescue. My nose runs and eyes water from the cleaning chemicals. Isaiah's sniffles having long ago dried out of tears. Fist on his hips, Dad nods and looks over the entire room.

"Well done Joseph and Isaiah," Dad says smiling for the first time tonight. "Since you both have so much energy, you can clean the kitchen, the bathroom and well who knows what else?"

I swear a good spanking would have been more merciful. Instead, Dad's wisdom causes us to suffer the longest night of restorative justice ever!

CHAPTER 16
SNAKE SCOTCHING 101

Isabella strikes again! She hogties Slim, pours rubbing alcohol on the dog, then lights a match. Dad gets there just in time. By experience and the correction of my father, neither Slim nor Slash raise up even a growl against Isabella. Dad being home is their lucky day. It seems that even in the animal kingdom Isabella is to be reckoned with.

Dad has no harsh words as he gets rid of Isabella's matches and fire-starting gear. "Slim will be outside" is Dad's only comment. But that was hours ago. Where is Dad now? When I ask, Paul scratches his head; asking Luke is like asking a stone. The girls have little to share. No one seems to know.

Meanwhile, Isabella is all fun and games. She and Isaiah are playing in the yard one minute and the next thing I know Isabella screeches past us. Isaiah, stick in hand, chases Isabella's siren call. Now he isn't one for much talk but the curses that burst from his little mouth could bleach a Rhinoceros' bones. Isabella is covered in bruises, mud and a crowning lump. I imagine Isaiah wields his blows smartly.

My baby brother's punishment for 'daring to whack' precious Isabella is measured in Mom's return of strokes. The tiny willow welts on Isaiah's arms and legs will go away soon. It is all I can do not to go to pieces with my arms full of quivering Isaiah. Besides, as-long-as I hold him it isn't too bad. I figure it is Mom's strategy more than strokes are which hurt enough on their own. Mom almost never punishes us. She wastes no time, however, dealing with the 'baby girl's' ills. I could swear, that on the way to her powder room, Mom is sniffling too.

Isabella is well cared for (no doubt) and at ease now in the house. She broods, half gloating as she licks her wounds. She drags her doll across the living room floor like the little goddess of victory. Her beetle-brown eyes are beams of pride. She celebrates her sins and insults, tricks and outright violence from basement to attic and from the family swing to the limits of the locked gate. But today, Isabella plays by herself.

"Roaming the earth like a roaring lion seeking..." Luke mutters under his breath on his way to heaven knows where. I grudgingly agree with his devilish quote. But Isabella and Luke are both unwanted 'angels,' far from paradise in my thoughts. Isaiah sniffles, cuddles, and the next thing I know I wake on the couch (still holding Isaiah) to the song of the kitchen bubbling, sizzling, and hissing. The air itself carries the full sweetness of the fixings: lamb, veggies, nutmeg, mint, cinnamon, apple sauce and other savors too. Dessert is going to be fantastic. Lamb--the main course-- one of Dad's favorites, and my least. I push Isaiah's sleeping form to one side of the sofa, get on all fours, and steal a peek in the kitchen.

"Daddy, Daddy," comes Isabella's voice. His back to the dining room, Dad strokes Mom's shoulder gently. Isabella tugs his pant leg. Dad tries to ignore her.

"Not now Pumpkin," Dad says gently to his baby girl.

"But Isaiah..." Isabella blurts out.

"Later!" Dad asserts and Mom anchors her arms around his neck as if to keep him floating away.

"I'm here for you baby. I won't go nowhere; clean bill of health. I told you. Young Doctor Siegel said it's just over-working; stress is all." Dad continues as Mom puts her head on his shoulder.

"Daddy, Daddy!" Isabella whines now tugging on his belt. "Daddy!" Dad just holds Mom swaying in place to a melody they alone share. Isabella turns in my direction with a look that could burn a hole in a stone.

"Don't you go to heaven without me Mr. Bookes," Mom says into Dad's neck. Isabella races by me as I hug the wall to avoid her touch.

"Stupid, stupid, stupid!" she rants half sniffling, paying me no attention whatsoever.

"Dinner!" Dad calls not too much later. Thereafter, the big kids aren't in the yard very long. The dining room thunders and rumbles under the oncoming family flood.

"Join hands," Dad says bowing his head. We look around, as some shrug and Isabella pouts. It's not a holiday, but I take Isaiah's outstretched hand. " 'The Lord is my light and my salvation- whom shall I fear?'" Dad looks around at each of us and draws a breath. I feel a sermon coming on.

"I thank you for reminding me how precious life is." Dad continues "My great-grandfather's, my grandfather's and even my father's heart failed them, but mine (praise you) is strong. Looking around this table, I know why, and I praise you all-the-more. Hallelujah and Amen!"

Mom beams, we echo the 'amen' and set to eating with motion as unnatural as green sunlight. Instead, and independently, everybody strains more to look at Dad than their plates. "I was at the doctor's office all day," Dad explains as I ease fork to plates, not knowing what else to do. Dad speaks little of adult business. I suppose he's telling us all now to ease Mom's uneasy nerves.

"Nothing serious, I just felt dizzy...and well...I went in for tests."

"Why?" Isabella blurts out, beaming a scowl then wiping the hand that Isaiah poisoned by his touch.

"Because my chest felt funny." Dad answers while cutting a quick look to Mom as Rebecca's fork falls to the floor.

"Oh, I'm sorry!" Rebecca announces loudly, leaning out of her chair to pick it up.

"That's OK," Mom says.

"Oh, look," says Rebecca," Isabella's shoe is untied. Dad, may we be excused? I can get a new fork and take care of Isabella's shoe too?" Dad nods. Up and away Rebecca goes firmly holding Isabella's hand. Ruth joins her sisters by taking Isabella with her other hand. I can hear the older girls whispering between gritted teeth as they jerk-drag Isabella out of the room. Dad clears his throat and continues eating. Moments later, frowning, Isabella comes back rubbing her upper arm; Rebecca and Ruth follow. The youngest girl's shoestring is still not tied.

"Mom?" Isabella starts.

"Yes Pumpkin," Mom replies without looking at her.

"What would you do if Dad died?" Isabella smirks. Ruth winces. Rebecca glares deer-eyed and Naomi lets out a little shriek. Struck silent, Mom looks at Dad for a moment as her eyes fill with tears not ready to fall. She scans the floor as if to find a forgotten answer at foot level. Mom rises from the table and all but tumbles out of the dining room.

"Honey, I'm fine!" Dad asserts as he gets up to follow. He didn't notice Isabella's evil grin widen. "Sweetheart," Dad continues in Mom's wake. One by one most of us leave the table and full plates. The table, plates and Isabella mind themselves.

Down from the living room to their bedroom, the sound of Dad's voice comes in a little above a sob, which opposes the scraping of Isabella's fork to plate. All but Isabella wait in the living room to try and make sense of it all. There are moments of fast whispering. The boys hole up by the doorway close to my room. The girls station themselves near the living room window. After their own whispering court, they walk over and join the boys' huddle.

"I once saw some fading telegram from the War Department in Mom's file box," Ruth says, "from the war Dad fought in Korea. According to Aunt Clara (who I talked to about it), the Army thought Dad was seriously hurt. The fact is he wasn't, and the telegram was a mistake. Even though the Army sent a correction, Mom was still rattled. A shock of this kind is probably always with Mom. I think Mom worries that Dad [or any of us really] might get hurt or worse."

We all drink in the information quietly. Having held that very old paper recently, I re-read each word vividly in my mind. Ruth is right. Mom is worried, with reason. This farm life and town aren't the easiest home.

Along about this point I notice, that Isaiah is out of ear-shot. He's picking Isabella's doll. In another moment he bashes it on the floor, wall and sofa over and over again. When Isabella looks to the clatter, Isaiah tosses the toy out of the window. The girl shrieks and rushes toward Isaiah only to stop cold and rethink her attack plan. I couldn't see Isaiah's face but his two clinched fists said plenty: He's mad! Isabella backs off. She is no match for his fists. I only follow out of curiosity.

"Stupid, stupid!" Isabella hollers and runs back through the dining room into the kitchen, past the mud room by the front door, and out of the house. Isaiah runs as quickly as he can and locks the door behind her. Isabella realizes the trick too late, when she yanks on the door handle. Through the viewport, I watch her rattle the screen door frame. The main door doesn't budge. Isaiah claps his hands and squeals with delight.

"Let me in! Let me in!" She pouts, then dashes her own doll against the solid door.

"Tarnation! What's all this fuss?" Paul asks.

"Nothing," I say stopping his hand from opening door. "Nothing at all." The more Isaiah's laughs roll, the more Isabella rants. Within seconds, she's kicking and smacking the door.

"Nothing?" Paul echoes and a light seems to gleam in his eyes. He and Isaiah smile. "Yeah, nothing!" He echoes.

"Quit making all that noise!" Peter (who shows up next) warns in an angry whisper. Neither Mom nor Dad seems to hear the racket.

"What are you talking about Peter? There's no noise." Paul says gleefully.

"No noise? Are you plumb loco! Isabella's banging on that door like the devil-hound is after her."

"Isabella? Who's that? I don't hear a thing. I don't see anybody at the door." Paul shoves the door open and nearly topples Isabella. "See," he says as he blocks her from coming in, "nobody is here at all." Isaiah squeals like he's in piggy-pie heaven.

Isabella is boiling mad. She rages, rants, and blinks back her glistening eyes, between inhuman howls.

"Stop that!" Isabella screeches as her first tears flow. "Let me in now!" Paul nudges Peter and continues.

"Nope, nobody is outside at all. It's just a bad wind. All the people who care about each other are in this house." Paul winks at Peter.

"Oh, I get it!" Peter says, spying on Isabella. "You're exactly right. There isn't anybody named Isabella in this family. And there never was."

"Stop that!" Isabella screams as Peter disappears into the house to return with all the other children...all wearing Isaiah's same goofy grin.

"Let's play a game outside," booms Paul's voice. We push by Isabella and make sure she can't get back in the house. Luke (blocks her) and leaves last so he can lock and key the door. Out of the corner of my eye, I see Luke pull the doorbell wire free from the buzzer. It's nothing for him to fix later, I'm sure.

"A game?" echoes Rebecca as if she's five years old herself. The family makes sure Isabella can't get past.

"Yes, the whole family will play. It's called? Wait, what is it called again?

"Invisible!" Isaiah pipes up.

"Yes, thank you, dear Isaiah. Invisible it is!" Paul says.

"I don't want to play," Isabella barks! "Let me in the house!"

"Did you hear something Luke?" asks Peter in a super silly voice.

"Nope, but I do smell a funny wind."

"Look what I found!" Ruth calls out ripping the doll from Isabella's trembling fingers. "It was just laying over here!"

"Give it back! Give it back!" Isabella wails as the doll gets thrown heavenward, then from sibling after sibling. Isabella makes the trip from brother to sister until both doll and baby girl reach Luke. Luke then tosses the doll onto the roof which ends its journey.

"Oops," he says clapping both hands over his mouth. When Isabella tries to escape, we force and drive her like cattle herding her back to the front stairs. We all use a bunch of stomps, rushes, and fake charges. Even though she falls a few times, no one touches her. Isaiah laughs himself to tears. Isabella's tears are very different.

For the next eternity of child time--ten minutes-- the baby girl cries, screams, kicks, and beats the door with her fists; she begs, wails and claws to no avail. Isabella throws fits and then has a full-on tantrum. She screams herself into raw-raspy breathing. Her voice gone; she shivers like wet pups in the wind.

Isabella's soiled clothing, messy hair, and reddish eyes make her look like insanity's personal poster child. Her sickly silence is broken by dry heaves and wild twitches that complete the crazy picture.

Inside the house, our living room curtain rises once then falls. A moment later, the front door opens. Starting with the oldest, Dad calls each of us by name. One at a time, my brothers and sisters stand before our earthly lord. Dad greets each of us with a grunt; we anxiously walk past the full-on man of the house. Sibling after sibling disappear into the safety, security and sanctity of our family home.

Dad calls my name and frowns especially deep. It's almost like he's saying, "I expected better from you." Dad stops calling just after calling the second youngest: Isaiah. As I look back to take Isaiah's clammy hand, we linger in the silence broken by one word.

"Daddy?" Isabella wheezes just above the crickets as her eyes plead and her trembling arms extend toward him. I suddenly know exactly how Isabella, Mom and the rest of us would feel if Dad were dead.

CHAPTER 17
SLEEPING-IN CLASS

Old Doc Siegel's assignments have me jumping out of airplanes, racing against time, beating super spies, and wrestling with a grizzly bear. My dreams have never been so much fun. I am their master now! No more night terrors shaking and screaming me awake. Just letting go is strange at first, but I'm getting more and more used to sweet dreams. I think Old Doc's sessions are as fancy as my dreaming. He's showing me how to direct my thoughts in ways I didn't know a feller could. What I mean is, I'm used to having nightmares so vivid, that in the short term I have trouble sorting them out from reality. But now, I wake up with good dreams still running.

Old Doc has me doing is front-loading my dreams. It involves a lot of fancy brain theory stuff that I'd rather not go into. It's the journaling that works. But it's not any kind of ordinary journaling.

Old Doc has me writing my worst fears into a journal book. The twist is I'm writing it all with the wrong hand: my non-dominant left, I'm a righty. It's a good thing I don't have Luke's handyman gift, or I'd have ability in both hands in no time flat. But for me, by the time I've scribbled anything out left-handed on the pad, I'm so frustrated about the writing process that I really can't focus on the bad stuff. I frustrate the process of focusing on bad stuff. I bust up the negative "ideation" as Old Doc says.

The other part of the assignment is to use my dominant right hand and write all the good things I'd like to do, get or be. Works like a charm! I have positive thoughts, supporting my confidence in writing and poof! I have a "dream script" that writes itself into my sleep.

Mom and Dad say I'm glowing now. In the last weeks, I've put on even more healthy weight and lost the dark rings under my eyes. I'm still skinny but have a bit more "meat on my bones" as Aunt Clara would say. I have never run faster, laughed harder, or had more joy in my life. I guess that's why I climbed the tallest tree on the place and stared out over the vineyard. I would never have tried that before, because I always felt like I'd fall. But confidence is liberating, dreaming or otherwise. Here I am laughing at the top of the world. My little brother just shakes his head.

I come down a few minutes later to find Isaiah shivering and crying violently.

"Three," he says.

"Three? I don't understand?" I say hugging his sobs away.

"Three!"

"Ok, ok," I say confused, my arms full of my little brother. It takes a while, but with the help of some lemon drop candies, a bit of yard running and so forth---Isaiah settles down. Not long after, he settles into a good afternoon nap.

I'm soon off again on my own adventure. I need to face more of these stupid things that used to scare me. Without a soul to lifeguard, I splash into the river and find no undertow, tentacles, shark-men, or fathom-phantoms to rip the life out of me.

I love my heart's racing excitement. I'm all jazzed up. I guess that's why I have this fearlessness. I mean, I go into the basement (to face darkness) without even a pause at the thought of eerie night stalkers hiding in their daylight haunt. Shadows have no power over me, now! I don't feel my background-fear of the dark or my dread of being alone. Old Doc Siegel has given me a new life all together. It's a life full of hope and facing challenges and taking them on with two fists. I like, love it!

Finally, I can take on the world! The chains of fear are off me! Maybe that's why I'm thinking of the white hangman noose. I still see it in my mind and need to do more than tie a yellow ribbon and give flowers to my enemies. Sometimes I hear the distant muffle of motorists on the roadway. I remember the saw damage to the Masthead and can't get it out of my mind. I can almost see the vandals coming back to finish the job. I recall Naomi's tears and triumph in patching and concealing the damage. She was really creative about it too. She patched and reinforced the one and then matched the black to the base paint of all six hollow Masthead poles.

I don't think the vandals like their nasty markings so quickly erased. I imagine the next attack will be with chain saws. But chains saws are too loud. Then I imagine the troublemakers bowling the sculptures over with trucks. But trucks will take too much effort to organize. That and trucks will take a long time to pull the poles down with. The vandals will likely come back and burn them. Fire is quick, easy and thorough. Not a lot of thinking, skill, or effort needed. I decided not to let the vandals do it. I have no wish to see Naomi cry. I will do something myself!

Since I really don't need too much sleep, I guess I will become a guard tower. This time, when the rope hanging, pole cutting fools come back, I'll be ready for them. This time, I'll stop them!

CHAPTER 18
THE STAKE OUT

It's almost nothing to convince Dad to let me sleep in the bunkhouse now. Mom still shows signs of worry but allows it. It's summer. A few days "camping" and it feels normal. After all, Horacio and Matteo, as well as our casual workers are there. The dogs are out. There are all kinds of guards to keep us safe. The distance from town keeps us safe from hateful eyes. The income from the winery keeps us safe from local finances, local politics, and local prejudices. Prejudices like what I see when I'm forced to take a few "non homeschool eligible" courses at the high school. Prejudices like all the kids in the basement workshop classes at the high school. In that school, it seems that every Hispanic, Black or dark-skinned kid is downstairs in the building's basement being taught basic reading and low remedial math classes. I guess they think we're all dumb.

I think it nearly killed the local district when I (once again), based on their test battery, excelled in aptitude. Their own system not only placed me in their high school but up at the advanced courses level; none of the collegiate-regent courses are in the ceramics, auto mechanics or wood shop. It seems like the basement—or so these nasty folk tend to think-- is the best place for "colored" people. That basement-thinking might be ok for Luke; his tinkering gift is well fed, but the other kids are just getting their minds filled with mold, fungus and mildew. Yeah, Mom's home schooling protects me. But when am I going to face those raw crazy parts of life for myself?

Our family, friends and even our workers keep us safe from dangers too many to count. Safe, safe, safe, we are surviving but barely living; not thriving at all. We get by and make ends meet and all that kind of stuff. We just don't fit in. Not really. We are in this place, but somehow not really part of it. We're here and nobody knows how to 'politely' or 'legally' get rid of us. We're here and dug in like a deer tick on a hunting dog. Yes, the bunkhouse is safe and a great place for me to light out from.

I have my regular sling shot. Dad took my compound slight shot when I cracked Luke's old football helmet. No, for the record, Luke wasn't wearing it. Anyway, the regular sling shot will have to do tonight. I pretty much have the yard to myself, except for Luke.

"Joseph!" Luke calls, "Joe, get me those pliers," he says without looking out from beneath the hood.

"Yes," I mutter and walk to him.

"Thank you," he says blindly reaching back for the pliers I press into his hand. I almost faint. Politeness isn't one of his strengths. "I really can't let go of this part right now. Bart's giving me $100 to rebuild it." Luke says excitedly without looking at me once.

"That's a lot of money," I say.

"Sure is! With this replacement truck, Bart will be able to pick up even more roadkill, discarded furniture and scrap metal," Luke shares gleefully. I'm happy about Luke's reward, but a bit worried about Bart having been here and gone without me even noticing. He's a ghost for sure. But then again, why be afraid of him? He's just a man, sort of. "Bart's odd jobs keep him fed. You know, he makes his living composting soil and hauling stuff for us. I'm glad he's a neighborly sort." Luke continues, and as suddenly as our talk starts, it ends. I leave Luke whistling some tune. I wonder when Bart will be back for this blue truck, but don't ask. One polite chat with Luke is plenty.

I spend most of the day getting ready for tonight. Something strong tells me that the vandals are going to try again and soon. Something inside me I have learned to trust. The last couple of nights at my guard post, nothing happened. But tonight, I just know something is going to happen. The last couple nights, I made this nest to one side of our entry. I sat still and just watched the road, the Mastheads, passing cars, and so forth. A deer even walked at arms' length past me last night. True to Old Doc's diagnosis, I can sleep and be aware at the same time. I don't understand the metabolism stuff, but I'm like the perfect--well rested--guard!

My nest is near the front gate and the damaged Masthead. It's a great place to see from and not get spotted. The big angel Mastheads Naomi created look solid but are made from this tricky kind of planking with the carvings on the outside. The Masthead poles are hollow. Dad secured each at the bottom with a metal eye beam which is then cemented into the ground.

In pairs, the six angel Mastheads face three areas. The two on the outermost part of the half-bowl-shape-turn-around are magnificent. They face each other with drawn swords held in folded arms. The two angels at the midpoint edges of the cul-de-sac are staring at the grassy knoll area. Their wings are spread back with swords ready to execute justice. The last two angels shoulder the dangling Bookes Family placard. Their wings, overshadowing the gate, look like the ones on the Arc of the Covenant. Beneath the wings, the family crest swings gently in the wind.

All six of the angels look like they could take off after somebody at any moment. They draw in the occasional passerby for Dad's wine samples, our grape pies, mom's soaps and lotions, as well as the girls' carvings, ceramics, and artwork. At times, the Mastheads have lured people in for Rebecca's handmade cards and painting as well. She is amazing. Truth is all my sisters are…even Isabella …but don't tell her I said so. Just the same, Naomi's wooden guardians all get their fair share of attention. I think the negative attention goes to the hangman noose on the oak; the pile of poop, at the bases of the Masthead, gets a less than honorable mention. I'd like to use some rope and beat the poop out of some vandals!

Well for another night, slingshot in hand I'm ready and it doesn't take long. I have my "Joe show" at the bunk house to arrange. I get in and bed down around 10 p.m. A few hours later, it's not hard to wake myself, since I'm not really sleeping anyhow. Sneaking out of the bunk house, down the road and easing into my nest is second nature. I've been blessed with light from a full moon.

The angel courtyard is lit up as though a healthy campfire is going. The mastheads are calming. At least that's how it starts. Somewhere between my lucid dreams rowing a boat onto Treasure Island with Long John Silver, I refocus on three dark shapes approaching from dry land and the main road. One of them is carrying a sloshing container. The wind carries the sweet smell of gasoline over the laughter of the moving shadows.

"You got that lighter?" a voice says as I hear a splash of gasoline on the damaged Masthead footing.

"Right here," another voice says. "We'll show them!" The voice says to an answer of laughs. I watch that one reach for something that turns out to be a lighter. Well, enough is enough! I fire slingshot marbles to yelping success and cursing responses most fitting for long seamen. "Not, my face, again!" howls my target. Before I can silently laugh and breathe in my victory one of the three moves a hand. A flash of light comes from it; there is a distinct 22-caliber pop sound and the leaves to the right of me rise and fall. I'm feeling like leaving my own pile of poop, right there. The figure advances and fires a second round. The bullet passes through the brush just feet away. I stay deadly still. Poop is about all I can do. Luckily, his shots are wild. There is no way he sees me. No way! But that doesn't stop the shooter from pointing exactly in my direction. I grit my teeth as to the right of me fire spits from the shadows, thunder bursts in stuttering peals, and the earth around the three would-be fire starters, erupts into puffs and plums.

I see the arsonist/shooter's pistol fly-fearfully from his hand, but other than that I couldn't tell you about the retreating vandals. I'm trying to run away myself, only to find I'm up in the air, on someone's hot shoulder and traveling like lightning --with a jingling sound--through the woods. A goblin has snagged his human dinner! Or worse; what does this kind of death look like for me? My new legs have no trouble doubling back onto the outskirts of the property to find the bunkhouse. The lift-body puts me down behind the now empty bunkhouse. I imagine everyone else is probably down the road by now.

"Don't take on more than you can chew, boy!" I hear Bart say harshly and clearly. I see him in a new way with his shiny M16. All my fear of him is gone. He's no longer the monster in the municipality; he's the guy who just saved my butt. Strapped to one side of the rifle is a smoky wire bag of (what I imagine are) expelled shells. "Get home," he grunts. I stumble back into the main house and Mom's arms. I'm not so sure if I need new underwear.

CHAPTER 19
GUARDED CONDITION

A bunch of soldiers and strange dogs on the place is my first clue that things are about to change. Dad--wearing both his holsters-- greets them without a smile. If they, my parents, were overly protective before, after the shootout they go into overdrive! Each soldier is identical: sack, M16 rifle, uniform, haircut, and boots; except 1: Bart. He stands a head taller and a plastic jaw from all the rest. Bandit style, the handkerchief covering the gaps in the fake jaw seems to speak volumes. What's worse, nobody leaves the place. It's a lockdown! I mean really. All this, one day after the police came. Dad keeps the police stuff to himself, but I kind of have an inside track on the whole thing. I get the feeling that nothing about our white noose party gets mentioned.

The place is a quiet buzz. For the most part, we kids get to watch from the windows. I expect a machine gun nest is getting installed with trenches and flame throwers. But what I get instead is a lot of extra vitamins, Mom's undivided attention, and a new stack of books to read. The books are a welcome (but brief) distraction. The children gossip all kinds of theories from aliens and monsters to Klansmen and Nazis.

Mom's worrying is the most annoying thing. She's the sweetest, kindest form of killer. By lovingly overwhelming her children, she kills all hope of fun and freedom. In fact, she can and does smother with affection. She doesn't know too much recent info about **it**, but she knows something. Trust me, mothers always do. They know when you've been sleeping, they know when you're awake. Santa ain't got nothing on Mom. Well, almost. I may not admit it, but eleven years old or not, it's still a comfort knowing she sometimes—when it's not Dad--sits in the chair next to my bed at night. Someone watching over me when I sleep is comforting. But I still have unfinished business. This lockdown is keeping me from finding out what's going on around me. That's not a good thing. Tonight, Mom watches me. After a few hours, she closes her eyes and nods off and that's my chance.

At about 4 a.m., I manage to sneak out of the house, more for my sanity than anything else. I might get lucky and find out what's been happening. Besides, there is only so much staring at the ceiling a fellow can take! A few steps into the yard, guess who I run into? Bart!

Without missing a beat Bart corners me, whips out –of all things--a necklace. "This cross is made from a bullet from that gun that shot at you last night; the bullet with your name on it," Bart whispers into my ear. "I doubled back and found the pistol." He says offering me a shiny chain. "Boy, take this and go back to bed!" Bart growls. I'm jumpy, but my skin does not crawl this time! His scarred face no longer scares me.

It's a cross. By the porch light, I didn't get too far after all. I see the amazing artistry. The cross does not look like a "your name on it bullet" at all. Other than the copper color, the flattened and reshaped shell casings look amazing. Bart has beautifully re-purposed a thing of death into a new life of its own. I think Bart could, at any festival or trade station, easily sell pieces like this. If I hadn't almost died to get one, I might have liked the present even more.

I guess I'm not biting off any trouble tonight. Apparently, I can dream anything I want, but living is something completely different. After I sneak back--past Mom—and into my bed, I wonder what's coming next.

CHAPTER 20
BEARING THE CROSS

    Bart gave me this millstone around my neck! A festive symbol for death and destruction: the cross. I mean for a bunch of flattened bullet shells is fancy. I can feel the etched grooves that meet at angles and make the joints look like feathers. The seams are welded and can be felt but not seen. The casings are flat with the ends cut to triangle shapes which are bonded together with the bullet cap dead center. It's light, airy, and pretty. The thing that was supposed to kill me, is kind of nice. But here I am spending far too much time toying with it. I'm still housebound and the reason the entire family doesn't go too far from the porch. I keep thinking about the 6'6" giant. Bart chucked me over his shoulder, and in full military pack, ran through pitch darkness, brought me home, went back, found the 22 pistol and is doing heaven knows what else at night. Bart has some kind of bounding barns in a single bound strength with Buffalo soldier night vision and a Zulu spirit guide thrown in for good measure.

    I guess the thing that is scary is his milk-jug jaw. Bart has this bandana-covered plastic chin. He has deep burns, scars, and canyon cuts across the lower half of his face. What passes for a voice is the type of growl that upsets alley cats. But that isn't, I mean wasn't, the worst of it. As big as he is, Bart can sneak up on rabbits. I think he can outrun rodents too. I can see why people fear him. I think I do still…though a little less now.

    Just outside the window, Dad is in the yard fussing with the Dobermans Slim and Slash. He has them turning, heeling, sitting running, stopping, and such. From the outside it looks like a man playing with his pets. I know different. Each animal is being given details and instructions. Dad is testing them. I've seen him work with dozens of dogs over the years. Every time, it's like watching Auntie Clara sharpening knives; slow-moving and deliberate. The blades, like the dogs, become sharp tools for thrusting or cutting. I can't imagine being safer. Though I'm a prisoner in my own house because of me, because of my over confidence and pride.

The other night someone was trying to kill me. Someone who is probably willing to kill us all, I guess. I got a piece of that feller with my sling shot, but he's gotten a chunk of my freedom in exchange. Dad with his guns, dogs and these military fellers, won't let harm come our way. I guess I'm still 'chewing' what Bart says I can't handle. I have my cross to bear too. It's in the shape of pride, anger, fear, and my inner voices. It's all around and inside me and forms me. I understand my confidence a bit better too. I should be confident. I should be carefree. I should be a child. But a piece of me can't. I have these above my pay grade kind of thoughts. I didn't sign up for any of this.

The side door bangs shut and Luke jets out into the yard, as if silently called. Dad pauses; the two exchange some words and I see Luke jump into, then start Bart's new blue truck, the one he was working on earlier. The engine sounds nice. Even I can appreciate the fine tuning of our mechanical genius. Luke is proud of his tinkering. Truth be told, if a thing has an engine in it, Luke can probably fix it. Moving parts are his artistry. It isn't long until the red hauler pulls up to the gate. The dogs can't hold back their enthusiasm. Bart drives into the yard, parks his truck, and is swarmed by man and beast. Luke and Dad exchange words. Bart nods and points off towards the west part of the vineyard. Dad and Luke nod, get into the red hauler and drive out the gate. Bart remains. He peers over the yard and house. Those tiny dark eyes drink in the farm.

I'm out the banging screen door, across the yard and to Bart even before the dogs take notice. My arms are around his middle. I'm hugging Bart! But he's different now. I let him go.

"Can you kneel, please?" I ask. He nods and I'm eye to eye with him. Bart toys with his blue hauler keys for a moment but puts them away. My hand traces the side of his head and the bandanna. I remove the cloth from his head. I investigate the strap of his plastic jaw. I loosen the contraption too; and he lets me. His eyes do not waiver. The dark scars and twisted skin are far from emptiness. There is a jaw beneath the plastic jug and a landscape with a man's face. "I'm not afraid of you anymore." I say to him.

"Good, not wise. But, good," says Bart placing his mask and cover over his jaw. "Good," he says again as I notice the silver necklace. At its base dangles a twisted-metal crucifix. Bart notices my new courage. "It's hair from the dog that bit me," he says.

"Hair, from what dog that bit you?" I say trying to imagine any dog that stupid.

"It's an idiom. This cross is made from shrapnel. It's the bomb metal that nearly killed me."

"The bullet with your name on it," I say.

"Yes," Bart says showing me the gun metal cross. "Yes. The bullet with my new name on it too." Bart says patting me on the head, tapping where my cross is, and straightening, just as Dad and Luke return with the red hauler. Dad isn't surprised that I disobeyed his stay 'in the house order.' Luke grumbles. I guess he's getting used to the favor I have with my parents. I go back to the porch and watch as Bart takes his new truck, and the red hauler gets parked to one side of the house. Luke starts his work on the red hauler. Dad walks directly to me.

"Come into the house," Dad says. I follow him silently. I can't tell where everybody else is, but Mom is reading. "Rachel, honey, come here please." He calls. Mom smiles, puts down her book, and joins us. Without a pause Dad reaches into my shirt and gently exposes my little cross. Mom nods as they both pull out their crosses. Dad's is made from some large bullet casing. I can tell because it looks just like mine except the size of the flattened casing and the grooves in his are spirals. Dad touches my cross as I study his. He looks away to Mom. I can tell they've been talking about me. My cross. I don't know what they're going to ask me. Dad doesn't say anything.

Mom moves closer. Her silver cross on the silver chain, a first glance seems normal enough. But it's not. The sides are thinner as they go down. It's made from stainless steel that's really shaped like a dagger point. At this moment I realize, Mom's cross is made from a pocketknife's blade. I've spent my whole life looking at these crosses and today I really see them. Dad and Mom don't tell me about the "hairs of the dogs that bit them; and I follow their silent example. I imagine the things that nearly killed them, which are now the very symbol for what makes them live. I feel my chest rise a bit in pride and fall even more in dreadful reflection. Mom rubs my head.

"Anything you want to tell us?" Mom, who's been almost completely silent until then, asks. I shake my head, too unsure of what to say. Dad grunts, "Go play with your brother," Mom says, turning a concerned look toward Dad. I slide into the body of the house recalling the gunfight. One of the gunmen's phrases comes drifting: "not, my face, again." The 'again' part lingers in the hazy half known air of my mind.

CHAPTER 21
ROD AND STAFF

It's been a full two weeks since the shoot-out and I guess Mom and Dad are easing up a little. I no longer have a chair bed guardian every night, and the children can play in the yard. Even better, I haven't seen, heard, or felt the 'military' for days. I guess the soldiers and dogs are all gone. The danger must be over. Dad has even put away his pistols. Though I keep fidgeting with the cross Bart made me. As much as I'm thankful for the shootout rescue, I'm just hoping Bart's not off the property. Saving my life makes me see Bart the man and not the creature. It's good that my folks are calmer too. I am happy. But, as usual, I'm still too young to appreciate my most recent mistakes; but bliss has its cost too.

"Stop playing!" Dad's voice commands over the horns and sirens. Isaiah and I stop. It is smart to listen. After all, the other children are still cleaning their rooms. This morning —with a cheerful voice-- Dad said, "clean your rooms." Naturally, Isaiah and I get to the business of sorting, packing, and organizing. It's old habit by now. It's also a lot like counting so Isaiah's favorite game becomes my pastime. Dad or Mom says, and we do! Not too much later when Dad announces, "Ice cream trip!" Mom couldn't care less. She re-reads a letter (about that old snake I imagine) from Uncle Solomon. The rest of my siblings all come running until Dad asks: "did you clean your rooms?" They all sadly (except the two youngest males) fade back into the inner house.

Dad's too old to be treated like a kitten. Shaking his head, he leads us to the sports car. This is one of his other treats, the re-built red show car. He loves us, but this ride has occasional favor too. Painful past experiences have taught my younger brother and I to move quickly and wait quietly. True, neither of us ever really knew exactly what Dad ever wanted from us (or was going to give away) at any one time; few of us ever figure him out and feeling more than thinking keeps us still; and I believe he likes it that way.

The open convertible roof forces the air into a funnel of cool fingers wiping hot licks of the sun from youthful brows; the car stops in front of *Jackson's Commercial Farm Gear/Bait & Tackle,* and we only dare to move a little. Jackson's meant crayfish, crawlers, minnows, lures, reels, rods, and the like. Clearly, Dad's getting his treat out of the way first. His glowing smile greets the only other adult customer; the stranger nods and turns his face away. Dad, still polite, gives him a second look.

It's not hard to notice folk who aren't from around here. They sort of stick out; and with this one, even I notice his baseball cap and dark sunglasses. Not much of a face to be seen. The stranger wears jeans and tattered sneakers; and he gives off a scent of shower free athletic endurance covered with cost-effective cologne. To make matters more striking, the stranger don't look like any fisherman I've ever seen.

Stranger or not, little brother and I are up, out and about the aisles laughing and playing seek and avoid (but not touching anything). You never touch anything without asking--- never, well, hardly ever. Even though I want the Chaucer III Professional Fishing rod right in front of me, there'd be no fish tales told with it (by me) today, I suppose. Apart from my fishing skills, I doubt if Dad's heart could be moved to buy it. The $50 rod is the most expensive one other than the ones in the case, behind the register.

"That's a nice rod and reel," I hear a joy and sadness in his voice.

"Yes, sir," I say to the smelly stranger.

"For game fish," the stranger all but whispers as his hand trembles. His eyes seemed steady fixed upon mine. He speaks almost as if he is somewhere else, talking at some holiday time; then just as abruptly, the stranger walks away, without another word.

I'm sure Dad is going to say "no" about me getting that fancy rod. I just eye it a bit like the stranger did. I know even touching the pole is stupid. Just ask Adam and Eve about the reward of their hands and desires; they'll tell you a real story!

Spying on the room without seeing Dad, means he might not see us. This kid logic is usually proven wrong, since Dad can sneak up on a rabbit.

"When, I tell you to go, then go." Dad says, as I suddenly realize he's standing right behind me! "Do you understand?" Dad whispers, grasping my shoulder and eying Isaiah. His voice has a hint of Mom-like concern. The hairs on the back of my neck stand up. Can Dad read my mind? Have I done something wrong? Did Isaiah? Lord!?! I nod and blink as Isaiah does the same, while the strange customer brushes by us again. The fellow smells like an exercise class gone on far too long. I suppose wearing a wind breaker in the noon day summer sun isn't any too comforting. Dad's eyes narrow; but before I know what I was saying or why I was saying it, I speak.

"May I have that?" I ask reaching across and taking hold of the fishing rod. Dad still strokes my head but is looking the other way.

"Sure," he whispers gliding with catlike ease to the store front. Why did I speak? Why did I lie? I didn't want anything, except this bad feeling to go away.

All at once Dad barks "Jackson!" and three things happen: the smelly stranger is taken from a drawn pistol, his footing, and consciousness. With his next move, Dad kneels near on the downed robber, takes his pulse, then opens the bandit's revolver's bullet chamber.

"Hey, Jackson, it's not even loaded?" Dad says spinning the chamber as the two conscious men laugh. Next Dad bellows, "kids, go to the car!" Wild hearts pounding, the two of us run. Are shoot outs becoming a new Bookes Family tradition? Meanwhile, the car was a gloom as police, an ambulance, and lots of others (don't know why they came), mill around the parking lot for what seems forever. Dad gets to talk to all these folks scribbling notes here, wiping his brows there, and whistling in amazement (like everybody did when I caught that Sturgeon last year.). And what comes naturally to two kids--quieted by adult business-- sitting in the back seat of a car? Play! Near death experience or not, none of my siblings could sit in the back of a car without giggles, slaps and funny faces. We did as we pleased until all the emergency medical vehicles and official folk go. The smelly criminal is hand-cuffed in the back of Deputy Thomas' speeding sheriff's car. The dust settles.

At the doorway, Jackson is all praises.

"Jackson, thank God and not me. The Lord sent me here 'for a time such as this.'" Dad says, but Jackson continues his praise and shoves all kinds of stuff into my father's hands. Humble or not, I don't think Dad could refuse some of Jackson's gratitude. Dad puts his gifts away. As we back out of the parking space, the car jerks to a standstill as he stares directly at me.

"Where did you get that?" Dad asks, pointing at the brand new $50 fishing rod and reel next to me.

"You bought it." His eyes dig in; my voice rises with my quickening breath and heartbeat. "I asked and you said SURE!" I look to Isaiah for strength as he slithers over to the other side of the car.

"I bought it?" Dad mumbles "I..." he pauses, looks away and begins laughing as he drives us home. I shrink into the seat. Laughter, I found out, rains its blows too.

CHAPTER 22
THE BEAR OF BABYLON

There we were staring death in the mouth (again) and this time not even knowing it! Local newspapers, radio, and T.V. sing my dad's praises for his 'singular heroism.' The media nicknames him: " 'the Bear of Babylon' a family man defending his children." Dad likes this attention about as much as I like being tickled after drinking too much soda pop. If you ever want to see me break somebody's nose, tickle me! Anyway, Horacio and Matteo don't like Dad to be on public display either; it doesn't tickle them at all. Horacio does it in words, Matteo in nervousness. Our newest family member didn't want to attend the event, or any kind of special award ceremony at town hall. I'm just glad there's not been said a word about my part in my second 'gun battle.'

The lone gunman (who is really old) in the bait store robbery is still recovering. Taking his meals through a straw, I guess. Anyway, if I want to see, I'd just have to walk down the last wing of the building. Our town hall is a one-shot deal, town hall, library, recreation, sheriff, and a small candy shop. It's kind of convenient that way. At least the crook has a roof and three square-meals now. But I can't help thinking there has to be a better way. I guess this was part of the gunman's plan. I remember the failed robber looking and smelling a whole lot of homeless. It reminded me of when Matteo first came to us; he also had the "outdoors too long" scent.

Like the prisoner, Matteo's gotten some surprising help. Unlike the robber, Matteo ran into the gentle hand of the Bear. Dad says, "there but for the grace of God go I," and that I shouldn't judge any man's stumbling. "People do a whole lot of things to get by." Papa says. "No son, the bullet-less gun, with the robber, tells the heart of the matter and man. That man hasn't got much but fear," I figure, if the crook's so down-and-out as to not have a house, home, or family, the empty gun makes sense. I wish my other shoot out gunman didn't have ammo; but this poor and smelly soul couldn't even afford or steal bullets. Heaven only knows how he got a gun.

Dad is getting some kind of 'town" award today. He won't tell us what it is. He just mentioned that it'll be "politically charged." This is Dad's way of telling us to be on our best behavior. Because at first glance, I can tell the public event hall is full of townies and outright snakes. These vipers are the "proper" folks who turn and slither their noses on the world, unless they get exactly what they want and when they want it. It's a 'photo opportunity' for them. I notice the closed and empty suite of the original health office. The Health Department now has its own entire and separate building courtesy of the Brummun family. It must be nice for old Phineas to buy a whole building for his brother Harlan. I'm thankful that Dad got to beat up at least one villain this week.

Babylon is so small that we have a Community Executive, instead of a mayor. I guess it's not a bad deal for an old strip mall gone sour and then 'rehabbed.' Matteo loves our library as much as I do. He hides in the air conditioning and all but inhales literature. As a result, his English skills are really improving. Mom is such a natural teacher. But Matteo's on a mission to master English. Every visit, Matteo and I don't know why, but we're fearful at the sight of barred windows of the sheriff's office and the small detention wing. The jail cells can hold maybe three prisoners like weekend drunks probably. Matteo won't talk about his anxiety. Matteo's silence does not quiet others. There's all sorts of adult talk blending together like buzzing-hissing bees and shopping mall noise.

The family is all dressed up as if they're attending an Easter parade! I can appreciate a child's dislike of fancy clothes. Matteo all but crawls out of his new suit. It's clear that this is his first store-bought jacket. It is equally clear that Matteo doesn't like the TV cameras. I notice Matteo repeatedly tying his shoe, turning away or outright being out of any camera frame...every chance he could. Matteo squirms in the two or three shots he can't avoid. I guess fancy events aren't standard affairs for street smart Mexican kids.

In his best Sunday clothes, Horacio stands proudly with his squirrelly nephew. Matteo, like our Horacio to us, is just grafted into the family vine. His real family (his mother anyway) works as a night club performer at some kind of hotel. I guess she sings because recently Matteo mentioned lady of the evening or some such thing. But no matter how many times I (or others) ask, Matteo claims he doesn't know his father. Out of goodness, Horacio takes care of Matteo. They are close and that's what matters.

Anyway, this here boring event is vexing my spirit. I mean we're all just standing here being stared at. I could slip into the library and at least get an adventure story. I just don't enjoy being in a room with the folks who'd rather burn us out than return a greeting. It's hard not to spit. Looking around the room, I figure, not enough crooks are jailed! Meanwhile, I hear Horacio 'Spanish language calming' Matteo who is all but shaking in his boots. I can't understand the words, but it's easy to read his concern.

"Philip Killdeer Bookes," Sheriff Witts all but yells toward the TV recording crew, "having priory completed a course of law enforcement study, served in the Armed Forces nationally as well as internationally pursuant to both civilian and military codes of the United States of America, is hereby enlisted as a voluntary-auxiliary police officer of the law for the jurisdiction of Babylon, conferred at the discretion of this office at this time and effective until further notice." The sheriff's speech and award of a police badge to Dad causes many to cheer, but not Matteo.

Matteo withdraws body, mind, and soul, during the open applause as he hisses:

"La policía?!? El hace de la policia? Part of the police? Your Dad?"

CHAPTER 23
ME, MYSELF AND EYRE

"Doc! Face what I fear most? What kind of research is this?" I blurt out.

"This exercise, and that's what it is; something to strengthen you. It's the next and necessary step, Joseph," says Old Doc Siegel as he rises from his chair. "You'll be fine. You're ready for this." He says smiling as he pats my head. "You'll be at our hospital, monitored by our best nurses & technicians, observed by sleep study specialists, and I'll personally be there to help, if you need it. But given your progress, I doubt you'll need any of us," says Old Doc. At the end of the session, I even get a lollipop.

Mom brought me to see Old Doc Siegel today, sometime after the second shoot out. Everyone knows my spectator role in the robbery. But since I don't think Bart has told anyone his part in the first one, I'm keeping my mouth shut. No sense surviving two-gun battles, only to get killed by my parents! Old Doc wants to keep me overnight and wire me for a sleep study. Mom has an odd faith in Old Doc's ways. Normally she has nothing to do with modern medicine, unless there's a crisis. For most things, Mom takes care of us, but this is a special problem, I guess.

Old Doc has been interested in me from the beginning. He says I am unique. Old Doc was the family doctor who revived me from my nearly fatal birth. Recently, sleep and reviving have become Doc's stock and trade. Old Doc went from one kind of medicine to another, in large part because of me. He has been studying me and my sleep issues for some time now. The hospital at the Reardon University of Science Health in Rochester is like Old Doc's live-in library. The air is pure to the point of bleached lifelessness. Why Mom wants me here overnight, and why I need to dream of what I fear the most is silly. I don't miss the nightmares. I don't see why I should revisit any of them. Now that I've learned to lock them out, should I let them back in? Crazy.

The round bandages on my head are cold and the wires scratch my face. It's the same with the gizmos on my legs, chest and sides. I feel like an astronaut. This is how they wire them guys up too. But instead, I'm going to inner space to fight the bogey man.

"Don't worry, Joseph," Old Doc says, "You're more than ready for this experience. You'll be fine," he says leaning in close, "**It** won't know what to do," he whispers. I wish I had his nerve. I keep flashing back to the bait store incident: the robber, Dad's Dambe Fu take down, the fishing pole, all swirling or squirreling (take your pick) in my head.

"I'm ready as I'll ever be," I say. Doc nods.

"Well then, clear your mind and take up your pencil. Good, that's good. Now write 'what I fear most' with your dominant right hand." He instructs.

"That's it?"

"That's it." Old Doc says as I stretch out on the white mattress." Give yourself the sleep command," he says. Doc really doesn't know how I instantly sleep or wake. Neither do I. I just sort of think it, and it happens. The scary thing is I can wake up at any given time like clockwork. I've got a chronological-mecha-ton inside my head! I guess that's a good thing. I wouldn't want to sleep entire seasons away. One of the things Doc says this research will be good for is possibly learning how people in comas can be revived. I don't get any of what he's talking about, but since it'll help Doc, I'll do it. I owe him that much.

So here it goes, eyes closed, toes relaxed and…I'm suddenly standing in a dark room. I can hear **it** breathing behind me. No, not this time; **it** is going down! I spin around fist ready and feel **it**'s fist. Stunned, I stare at my own face and hit the ground, not moving. I've knocked myself unconscious in my dream. What's worse; none of my wakeup tricks are working! I try but I can't rouse myself. I'm like a helpless piece of meat lying on the plate waiting for the hungry dinner 'guest' to arrive.

"We give you the power to wake up now," says an all too familiar voice. Feeling my jaw, I open my eyes and find myself face to face with 10 young people. "I knew you could make it," one of the voices says as he offers me a hand. I look at the group. They are too familiar; 10 young boys and one baby. The kid offering me a hand up off the floor is a slightly 'skinnier' me?

"What's going on?" I ask him…me.

"Oh, that's easy," this one says. "I'm Ten."

"Ten?"

"Yes, Joseph at age 10; ---you from last year. You see these are Nine, Eight, Seven, Six, Five, Four, Three, Two, One, and the baby Zero."

"This makes no sense!"

"Well Eleven, it makes perfect sense. We are all me and I am you.

"Who knocked me out!"

"You did. Or rather you will. That was/is/will be you at age 12. Thankfully Twelve is stronger than you."

"What?"

"Well Eleven, since you don't get it, I'll have to explain. Each one of us is you at a different age or at least the feelings, emotions, and instincts you had at that age."

"Go on Ten," I say feeling my jaw burning.

"You have a near perfect memory and that extends down to your feelings and instincts." Ten pauses and puts his/my hand on my shoulder. "I see you're still confused," he continues, "your worst fear is dying alone in your sleep."

"That's **it**." I say.

"Here we are," Ten says.

"What?"

"It should be clear to you by now. There is no **it**." Ten says smiling.

"No, **it**?"

"None, but our time is short, so we need to get right to it, Ten says. "Hold the baby."

"Ok," I say feeling like there are ants crawling all over me. I don't know why, but of all the numbers of me, the baby is the one that "creeps" me out the most. Well that and Twelve. I want to have that kind of a punch!

"Here," Ten says as one of the other kids places Zero into my hands. "Zero is pure instinct, but he knew Joshua."

"Joshua, my—our-- twin who didn't make it?"

"Not exactly, nine months of Joshua are with Zero and as a result with all of us."

"But how?"

"Womb-mates dude. Zero can't talk but can you feel his experience, his instinctive muscle-memory?" Asks Ten.

"Yes," I say. "I feel warm and safe and the whole universe is Joshua and me. It's so happy. It's like heaven."

"That's what killed Joshua. He didn't deal with the real 'not heavenly' world you were born into. He went into fatal shock and withdrawal from the hostility and coldness of the outside world. He died rather than leave us."

"I…we killed him?"

"No. His will did him in," Ten says and Zero wriggles. "Joshua refused the world," Ten says. "Joshua went back to before there was a full Zero for him," Ten pauses, then takes a deep breath, "but that's not important." He continues, "What is important is what we need to share with you right now. All numbers here, touch Eleven," Ten commands. All their feelings wash over me. "Eleven, while you are age 11, you're carrying all these instincts, feelings, and emotions with you. Keep us with you. Don't trust any one of us all at once but use us." Ten says.

"But haven't I?"

"Not when you shield the dreams we're sending you."

"The night terrors?"

"Yes."

"But why?"

"Because without limits you jump into rivers, climb tall trees and stand in front of people trying to shoot you! You have misread our warnings and your limitations. You'll get us all killed…like Joshua you're trying to shut down the over-stimulation.

"I'm not suicidal!"

"Not at all. You need to listen to your instincts and use us and your wisdom at the same time."

"I thought that's what I was doing."

"What you were doing by shutting off the dreams is the same thing as shutting off your pain senses. How would you know something was wrong if you couldn't feel the flame burning part of you?"

"You're warning me?"

"More like cautioning you. Listen to us because the joy of childhood is surviving its foolishness. Right now, we need to tell you that you're acting like a fool."

"But I…"

"Shut up! Listen. We need you and you need us. Especially, if the number of us is to grow, you must grow."

"Aren't I?"

"Yes. If you'd have knocked out Twelve, we'd be dead now."

"How is that?"

"Well, each one of us, Zero and up gets wiser and stronger. If a younger number defeats the older you, well that's bad."

"Twelve is already here then?"

"Not fully yet. But if you listen to us and 'be you and observant' we'll all live in you, with you, and through you."

"Sort of like the Father, Son and Holy Ghost,"

"Sort of like maturity of mind, body and spirit. If you don't resist aging, you'll get wiser and we as a body will get stronger too. The 'night terrors' won't be necessary, if you act like you have some sense in the first place. Stop tempting fate!"

"Should I hide in the cellar?"

"No. Not at all Eleven. Be brave but don't tempt fate on a whim. We'll warn you, if you try."

"You see how well that's been working."

"Ok, let me rephrase. You make good choices and do what comes natural for your mind but use wisdom and like God-Uncle Solomon says 'discernment.' Go right ahead and jump into life, just not into the river. Brave can be fearless, but it shouldn't be reckless. One kind we live through; the other kind gets us dead," says Ten and the ground begins to shake.

"Ten? What's happening?"

"Twelve is happening. Goodbye Eleven, see you in your less terrifying dreams…if you behave."

"Bye Ten, Nine, Eight, Seven, Six…"

"Hi there!" my mildly deeper voice pipes up.

"Twelve?"

"Yup, the Ghost of Joseph future. Wakey, wakey! By the way, your jaw hurt my hand!"

"Good!" I say and we both laugh.

"It's going to be fun being you," Twelve says offering me a hand up from the ground in his consciousness.

"Any words of wisdom?"

"Nope. Just an observation about Isaiah," Twelve says. "If my read of Zero's feelings is right, your Isaiah is a lot like our Joshua. He worries too much about you. Calm him when you can. Oh, and that stake-out thing was stupid." Twelve cups his chin with his hands and continues, "Ask yourself, is it possible that Isaiah has a hidden prophetic gift?"

"Maybe old man, just maybe." I say as Twelve runs his hand over my head.

"Yup, I'm going to like being you," we both laugh again. The next morning, I wake up from my inside walk-a-bout with Old Doc's college sleep experiment, still laughing.

I bet the technicians don't know what to make of it all or of my EKG data.

CHAPTER 24
RUN OFF DREGS

In my life, with ever present death, pain, fear, and loss, there is never a dull moment; no sir, not for me. I barely have time to think about **it**, me, the dream inside the dream-thing, and the 'me' others, before the next little adventure rolls up on me.

Bloody and shirtless, Matteo rolls into our yard with what is left of his monster bicycle. The mass of twisted metal, torn flesh and turf grass, seem like one blended mass. Without a word, Matteo falls one way and the mess of a bicycle the other. Isaiah runs for help.

Between the peroxide and water, Hannah tweezes raspberry cane-thorn after thorn from Matteo's bare skin.

"No, hospital! No burocrata." Matteo hisses. He looks like he's just lost a fight with a giant porcupine. His sides and back are peppered with thorns all the way up and down.

"We got to take him to a hospital Hannah," I say.

"He ain't legal," she says, as if I should know what that means.

"No burocrata, no polizei, no clinica! If they find me, I don't go back. Never!"

I stare at Isaiah who stares at me. Go back? Back to Mexico? I guess. But how does going to a doctor get you tossed out of the country?

"Boys," Hannah says "it's like this, he wants no official records on him, so let him be. Truth be told, I don't want to be 'found' and sent back to Pennsylvania either. These here new marks on Matteo are just like my old ones," Hannah sighs as Matteo nods and smiles a little between winces. I know both

Hannah and Matteo escaped bad people, so the answer satisfies…for the moment.

"Three shining motorbikes!" Matteo snarls at the rubbing alcohol, "Imbecil! Tres burro! Laughing, they run me off the road: cherry red, sun yellow and carrot orange motorcycles. All seemed like new toys."

"Three?" Isaiah whispers into my ear, later that day.

"Three," I repeat pressing on Bart's cross through my shirt.

"Three," I repeat and Isaiah nods. I still have no idea what it means and that scares me. True to his word, Matteo, for three days, won't give in at all: no Clinica! Horacio, Mom and Dad worry. Matteo shows more concern for his monster bicycle. It was because of the bike that Matteo is free. He is pretty emotional about his wheels. The bike made necessary Dad's and Horacio's New York/Mexico road trip-rescue. Prior to his rescue, good old Matteo just rode himself across the Mexican border --newspaper delivery boy extraordinaire-- and made a good three or four hundred miles, before finding a way to call Horacio.

Personally, I don't see why it's any problem since North America and South America are just like Canada and Alaska; it's all connected and might as well be the same country. During our family's past trips to Niagara Falls, all I ever needed to cross into Canada was my birth certificate. The border guard never checked. I do understand why Matteo doesn't want to go back to the "bad" people –who probably hurt him-- in Mexico, but why is he afraid of people here? We're not going to hurt him…except maybe those three motorcyclists on the shiny new bikes.

Anyway, Matteo uses Dad's fancy torch to repair his bike. He has free reign on tools, and has the talent to back up the liberty. Matteo's opinion is unchanging about the hospital. Horacio's tough wisdom, Dad's clear logic and Mom's gentle ways, move him not at all. Wincing through his chores, gritting his teeth to move, Matteo masters his pain. Hannah alone tends to him. Mom is great at her family craft, but Hannah has a touch that brings Matteo to rights. Our Hannah has the loving touch too. Since Hannah's two children and toddler, all but live here, it works. She's still plucking thorns from his flesh and scalp. Matteo's back has whip marks (like those in old slave pictures.) These are crisscrossed with as many black-pit marks. I can't imagine being burned by cigarettes. Hannah seems to understand Matteo; their mutual, but respective pain.

Late evening of day six, Dad greets Old Dr. Siegel at the gates. I didn't know the sleep specialist made house calls. Old Doc retired from regular medicine to become a head-shrink doctor at Reardon University. He hasn't given me any new dream assignments lately. I think he's still trying to understand my EKG and the dream inside a dream.

"Hey John Sr., I have your special spirits in the rear near the water wheel." Dad points towards the rear yard. Old Doc grunts.

"Another galloon, I trust, Phil?" The two shake hands and I don't think a thing of it, since playing kick ball is more fun. Hannah, her children, and most of us are having a good old time. Matteo is in the backyard working on his mangled bike. I also didn't notice Siegel carrying his old doctoring bag with him. Well, a few moments later and I get to hear some powerfully nasty Spanish…the kind of sailor talk aboard the S.S. Madre! Matteo comes wheeling around a corner and almost just as fast, Hannah's arms are around him.

Old Doc catches his breath amidst the dust storm while a twisting, squirming and writhing Matteo all but cries. Not a tear leaves his face, just curses that I hope to never hear again. Hannah

114

holds him throughout, trying to cool his temper. The pair are standing and rocking back and forth in what looks like a tree leaning one way then the other with the changing breeze. Finally, Old Doc (who's peeled off all the bandages) nods, and applies clean dressings.

"You've got some fine recuperative powers, young man. If I didn't know any better, I'd say you've been healing for much longer than a week son," says Old Dr. Siegel, patting Matteo's undamaged shoulder. "Young man, I'm a semi-retired country doctor and since I'm just observing, unofficial like—and you're on the mend—, we can forego paperwork; but," Old Doc looks to Hannah, "call my son--immediately-- if he gets worse," says Old Dr. Siegel, as he's preparing to leave, with some of Sheriff Witts' German jet-fuel: Schnapps liquor: which when lit at night burns a royal-blue hue.

Next, Old Doc whispers something to our young Mexican. Matteo releases Hannah and embraces Old Doc. This time Matteo cries. Hannah cries, my sisters cry and Mom fresh from snapping green beans cries too. Dad clears his throat and turns away sharply to pick up Old Doc's special alcoholic spirits, I fancy.

Long after the sun goes down the crickets and cicadae chirp their chorus. Matteo, Isaiah, Hannah's eldest son Alvin all sleep protected by Mom's buggy oil and the mosquito-screening on the porch. Come morning, a new black & silver mountaineer bike (bells and whistles included) rests on the door stoop. The fancy lettered note simply reads "Matteo: Heart of Fire: this is home where you belong and will stay!" All the children give a nod at the spot-on-way Santa Claus surprises us with a mid-summer delivery.

I feel the little ones imagining ways to get some early Yuletide action. After all, who else --but a spirit--could get past guard dogs Slim and Slash? Meanwhile, I vaguely recall a nighttime whistling-wind sound. But currently the smell of freshly deposited deep ebony-soil holds me captive.

I feel an old familiar chill having little to do with Christmastide weather.

CHAPTER 25
FOR WANT OF KINDNESS

Now that colder handed John Roderick Siegel Jr., M.D. and General Practitioner is done poking and prodding, I can at least get home and enjoy part of the day. I prefer the practice of Old Dr. Siegel. At least his hands are a little warmer! Now that I'm done with Doc Jr. I can relax. Maybe even peg a target or two with my sling and marble-shot. But Mom didn't like the spots on my throat or my bout with thick red-mucous yesterday. I guess blood, any blood, from her children upsets Mom to the point of pestering Dad and here I am, 'burócrata! clínica!' as Matteo would say. It only hurts when I move, talk, laugh, breath, or cough. The dizzy light-headedness is a bonus.

The task of driving falls on Dad, since he is heading that way. I don't mind his company. Dad speaks little and fusses almost not at all. Silence is the habit of a man who's taught himself and made his own way through God knows what; neither the earthly nor heavenly Father will tell me Philip Killdeer Bookes' secrets. Dad's past is a mystery but give it time. What I do know is simple. Bloody knee, bug bite or scratches, usually get a splash of water and a hardy "go make play." Dad regards the sore throat much the same. But Mom, in her womanly wisdom (which I won't question), gently redirects him and…well. I hand Dad the medical caution and my prescription paper. I don't think I'll be drinking hard liquor, driving or operating heavy machinery any time soon.

On the way out of Thompson's Drug store, Dad pauses to feed dimes into several rows of candy machines. I wonder why he's giving away candy surprises to strangers. Anyone who happens to check the dispensers gets a gift. But he continues loading. Dad, who no doubt reads my face, pauses, then rubs my head.

"Joseph, the good you do for yourself dies with you, but the good you do for others is immortal," Dad quotes from his memory—but I can tell it's not Scripture. His secret Santa task complete, Dad nods once. "Since you not dying yet, I figure ice cream is a good enough medicinal?"

"Yes sir," I say, my hand in his. I ain't too old to hold hands, yet. It's not such a bad day. All the same, I wish I could hold off being sick.

The Heavenly Flavors of the Rainbow and its owner, Mr. Able, have no problem allowing free ice cream samples along the way toward a final choice. I'm researching the butter pecan and vanilla peppermint. Dad, practical man that he is, gets a double scoop of chocolate. It's not all that bad, being partially sick except for the full speed motorcycles bobbing and weaving through traffic. Dad shakes his head. No patrol car or Sheriff in sight; and I can tell Dad wishes for a giant fly swatter.

"They're going to hurt somebody," Dad says motioning after the trio.

"Or themselves," I pipe up. Dad shakes his head.

"Nope. Flashy folks and drunks usually hurt others," he says with a sigh; I sigh too tasting Butter Walnut Pistachio. We make it back to our truck, the hardware and tackle shop, attend his list, and head out. "One more stop," Dad announces. "I'm feeling like a DD Burger." I nod and the next thing I know, we pull into Danbee's restaurant parking.

It's been a while since Hannah's van smashed that deer outside Danbee's; now that she's employed here, we come more often. My joy, however, is short lived. In the parking lot, I spot the three motorcycles: a glimmering cherry-red one sandwiched between a sun yellow and a carrot orange bike. They are all sparkling factory new. Not at all like the local Rhodes Riders loud-dirty Hogs (big motorcycles driven by people who look lost from a renaissance festival.) These bikes aren't Hogs but oversized mosquitoes driven by boys who look like they wear make-up.

As we enter, Hannah smiles at us as she pushes a man's hand from her hip.

"Don't be that way honey," he says, and his two friends laugh. The feller, wearing all red, looks up as Hannah steps away. On my way past, I see the same three with matching designer leather gear, fancy pants, helmets, gloves, and accessories: red, yellow & orange respectively: townies to the hilt.

"Is you alright," Dad mouths to Hannah as she walks up to a low set table and seats us; my back is to the window while Dad faces the three.

"I can handle them," Hannah growls as she whips out her ordering pad and pen. "Your usual order, men?"

"Yup, coffee and the DD (Dan-Dandy) Burger for me but chicken soup for the boy," Dad says. "Joe has a sore throat."

"Poor baby," Hannah says and bends to hug me as I hear a catcall. After she stands back up, she rolls her eyes at the fancy-dress bikers. Dad grunts.

"Come on honey, share the love," Red Rider hollers to the laughter of Yellow and Orange. Hannah gets herself together, places our order, and ignores the heckling. Old man Danbee waves from the kitchen beyond the counter. I imagine he's coming through the large flapping door to 'jaw jack' with us. There are only two other customers. But to my surprise, Danbee Sr. doesn't move. Hannah's smile is more a smirk as she does her rounds.

"Hey honey cheeks? What about me," says Red Rider. Hannah refills coffee. I watch the counter mirror and see Red trying to slide his hand around Hannah's waist. "Hey, I'm not all bad," Red quips to the delight of his giggling goons. She avoids him by going to other patrons near the front door: refills, chats, laughs, and starts back toward the counter. I hear her stutter-step near Red (I imagine.) I turn around after a clear fleshy slapping sound. Hannah scoots forward at the smacking sound on her back side.

Dead silence: her smirk is gone. She takes about five more steps away as Red Rider stands up in pursuit. "What does a guy have to…" he tries to say something as Hannah turns; running and leaping right cross, elbow and shoulder smash combination into Red Rider's face; now, that truly shocks Red! As she lands pummeling Red Rider, Yellow stands. My slingshot drops Yellow Rider (and his knife) onto a scrambling Orange Rider.

"My face again!" Yellow Rider squawks.

"That's enough," Dad roars, extending the sheriff auxiliary badge in his left hand; his hand right firm and ready on his holstered sidearm. Danbee Sr. swings the service door: pump shot gun in hand. Wide-eyed Hannah moves out of the firing line.

"Do you know who I am!" Red yells cupping his own bloody nose.

"Fendrick, Terrance, and Reginald Brummun," Dad says flatly.

"My Dad will…" Red Rider starts.

"Find out that an 11-year-old boy and a 110-pound girl beat the tar out of the three of you?" Dad interrupts Hannah, Mr. Danbee's and my chuckling. The other two patrons are nowhere to be seen. I imagine they scrambled through the door a while ago. "Do me a favor boys," Dad continues, "I'd hate to have to write a 'shots fired' report. Now the three of you just mosey on. Leave the knife! By-the-way," Dad finishes. He has not smiled once; nor does he say a word about my participation: my re-loaded and ready slingshot.

Yellow and Orange right themselves and help Red.

"This ain't over!" Yellow says with his hand over a certain marble-mark; by way of answer, Danbee Sr. cocks his shot gun. The Brummun boys exit Abbott and Costello style, then Dad smiles some more.

On the way home, Dad laughs and musses my hair. I don't reckon the Brummun boys are anonymously gifting candy machines on their way to Dr. Seigel's office.

Man! I wish Matteo were here.

CHAPTER 26
THE PERFECT PHOTO-SHOOT

The grey sedan sits outside our front gate with the white shirt Caucasian taking pictures through a long lens; telephoto, I think. Dad whittles and ignores him. Mom shells peas and prays. And Matteo stays well out of sight.

"I guess Phineas Brummun didn't like Hannah's misdemeanor harassment accusation or my officially documenting the incident," Dad says out of nowhere.

"I reckon not," I say pegging another empty bean can from 25 feet.

"I just wish you could have been in the hearing room listening to them snakes deny, and cheat and lie until that knife, full of Brummun boys' fingerprints, was produced by yours truly." Dad smiles, studies his carving, then continues, "for which I am mighty thankful for the State Trooper's evidence lab, for expediting and returning."

"Does that mean the punks are getting jail time?" I ask hopefully.

"No, it just means I keep my Auxiliary Sheriff's badge. The Brummun family (young and old) are gunning for me. Since I lawfully displayed and used my credentials, and didn't threaten the use of force, the Brummun clan only hurt themselves by lying. They--for some odd reason--didn't mention the 11-year-old marvel sharpshooter." Dad gently cuffs my shoulder and I smile right proudly. "It also means that Hannah and Danbee can pursue civil charges if they want to. But they most likely won't." Dad shakes his head.

"Why not?" I ask.

"For one thing, I keep the auxiliary (which was in question during the hearing), besides, there's no sense in being a sore winner. And it's an expensive process and no real penalty--other than a fine or two. The Brummuns' recent perjury speaks volumes about their character."

"Good enough?" I ask.

"Good enough, I reckon; the hearing embarrassed the Brummuns. But this here photographer feller," Dad points at the car again, "is somehow connected to some new mischief. I don't want you mixing in it this time," Dad chides.

"Yes sir. No sir. Not me: unless" I say.

"Unless what boy?" Dad eyes me.

"That feller goes to touching somebody and…"

"That'll be enough! There's a reason you only got that there slingshot. I wear the pants around here! Not you. Not yet."

"I know. I know I got a lot to live up to," I smirk. Dad fusses my hair and shakes his head.

"Your God-Uncle Solomon's right about you. Too much like me," Dad smiles and continues whittling as I proceed with my miniature artillery. "Speaking of your God-Uncle, he is on his way here. We have some business to attend to, and I don't need you snooping around. When we're inside, you and his family need to 'go make play.' Am I clear?"

"As clear as a church bell, sir," I say, pegging another tin can at 30-feet. God-Uncle Solomon arrives with a truck, equipment and two fellers I've never seen before. Dad settles and dismisses the dogs to the side garden. They trot off, still watchful from behind the tall, cool weeds.

Luke almost falls over when Solomon hands him an extended use *Super 8* camera. That boy has been drooling over that thing since he first saw one six months ago. I guess God-Uncle got a new one or something. I can't quite hear what he says to him, but Luke is loopy. Solomon greets me with a hearty handshake, and a "my you've grown," then walks into our house with two big men carrying a rectangular crate labeled *Reprographic Process Field Kit# 18*.

Not a single child is in the house now. Luke calls me over. "I'm going to spy film that car guy," Luke says as I nod. Don't know what Luke wants me to do, but I watch as he walks through the kitchen garden and disappears beyond the corn stalks. I figure he's going to loop around and sneak up on the sedan. But there's one problem. The Sedan Guy's not in the car and after a moment or so of looking, I see him walking up the road clicking pictures. Upon his return, Sedan Guy grunts and heads for the front gate.

"Mind if I come in?" Sedan Guy asks?

"Yes, I do mind," I reply, as all the children but Matteo (who is probably watching from a hiding place) drift toward the gate.

"That's not neighborly," he says clicking a few more photographs and putting his hand on the gate-clasp. "Go and get your parents," he commands.

"Why don't you just go away," I say just as Slim and Slash slide silently to either side of me. Click, click, goes the camera.

Then his hand hesitates on the gate-clasp. "Go away mister, because I don't know how to call these two off if you unfasten that gate." I fill my lungs and make a guttural sound; the dogs sit. "In fact, I can't control them at all!" I continue to lie to Sedan Guy. As I snap my fingers; they lay down. "I can't even command them to ATTENTION!" They stand and growl outright. "Mister, for your safety, I'd recommend you stay where you are," I warn. He moves his hand away from the gate. Out the corner of my eye, I can see Luke filming. Sedan Guy backs up and fiddles with his camera.

124

"Maybe you can tell me where that Mexican boy is?" Sedan Guy says raising his camera with a burst of clicks. The next burst back peddles us all. A gun shot, a camera exploding, and all at once dog, man, and children scramble for cover!

Well, Sedan Guy beat it out of there so fast as to leave the camera causality, road rubber, and a personal puddle. Dad isn't happy. Kids are in the house, low and away from the window. Dad grabs, seemingly from nowhere, his Range-Rifle and a belt of bullets. Touching guns is a no-no. Handling Dad's Korean War Range Rifle is a never-ever.

"Stay down and away from the windows!" Dad barks. I've only ever seen that look in his eyes at the Bait Store robbery. Mom handles handfuls of trembling kids showing a bit of her own shivering. Soon, Dad's face softens as he makes eye contact with Mom. She nods and Dad's grim face returns.

Dad fingers free a few floorboards and slides out --under what must be-- the side porch. He resurfaces next to the first kitchen garden. Unbidden, from my perspective at least, Slim and Slash arrive. They're on patrol, I'm sure. Will people ever run out of bullets!?! If Dad catches whoever was shooting at us, there will be little need of a trial. Anyway, I can't see beyond the forbidden window; and wisely, I slide into the body of the house where Solomon is calling the local police.

Within 20 minutes both man and dogs come back; a hunt without much success. Dad holds a thumb-sized piece of smelly black rubber in his gloved hand.

"I filmed it," Luke squabbles.

"Good. It looks like you get to keep that camera, after all," Solomon says patting him on the back. I figure out that Solomon's two workers continue non-stop taking their own pictures of letters from Dad's office. Not too long after, the yard is full of State

Troopers, the Sheriff, and Auxiliaries; and to think, it only took the authorities 30 minutes to respond!

Still trembling, Sedan Guy-- in his new dry pants-- isn't quite so cocky now.

CHAPTER 27
MESSAGE AND MUSIC NOT FROM KANSAS

Dogs whining and smoke bubbling from beneath the ground is our first sign of trouble to come. We were already expecting a storm. Just the same, all work on weather-proofing the house stops. We take a chance at hope against the darkening skies that the leftovers of hurricane Dorothy --like the weather man said-- won't get here for a few more days.

In no time, Dad and the boys uncover and dose the fire in the old root cellar. It was smoldering black. Too much oil and sulfur in the spirit candles. Barring the supernatural, I guess, someone wasn't very careful. Poorly made candles could explode after a fashion. But, more than likely the lit candle was forgotten and that is what set something else in the root cellar on fire. Only a month ago, there was melting snow on the ground; now, the fire is twice as curious. Later that evening, I found out from Peter that the root cellar was lined wall to wall with dolls; and not the kiddy-kind. At that moment though, I see Dad piling the idols in the burn barrel.

"Ninety-seven dolls," Isaiah whispers with a hint of shakiness in his voice. I am wise enough not to question his math...ever. We each got a close but quick peak as Dad goes back into the cellar for more junk. I notice each corn-husk doll wearing bits of cloth, hair, paper, and so forth. Painted white, the ugliest is short, round, with one continuous bushy, black eyebrow. Three pencil thin dolls wear cigarette butts and a strip of red, yellow, and orange, each and of their own; one of the colorful three has a bit of white rope. In general, each corn husk doll is full of pushpins.

The stash of bleached animal bones, paper strips, rags, and doll parts is huge. Mom observes in grim silence as Dad burns the evil dolls. We watch the fire with a mixture of awe, concern, and wonder. I notice all eyes beaming curiously except my youngest sisters. Isabella has the knit brow rage of a Christmas morning met with the wrong toys.

Voodoo is a word rarely used in the house, since Mom and Dad are not at all into the idea of magic: white or black, good or evil, fair or foul. They are quite Biblical on the subject and I for once I agree. No other worldly powers need to be welcome around here that aren't expressly from heaven. However, the 'townies' love to throw that voodoo term at us and all our doings, especially Mom's herbalist, goodwife and midwifery callings. I guess since we are some of the few Negro-folk here-about, simple-minded 'townies' find nasty things easiest to believe. They probably think we're from 'the Voodoo Isle!

What the small-minded folk do know about us is that we are immovable. Try as they might, we aren't budging! Over the years, since we got this place, we have been blamed for crop failures, sick children, warts, ingrown toenails, and even missing pets. Given Mom's and even my knowledge of plant remedies, it would be easy to bring a poison-plague or two on the locals. But we don't. For the most part, our real friends let us know what the 'townies' say, and where possible what they are up too.

Chief among these 'townie' types is that varmint Harlan Brummun; the Health Department phony, who no doubt, wears Italian white and alligator shoes even before May. I'm sure, based on seeing God-Uncle Solomon's recent legal actions, that the Brummun clan is somehow involved. Don't get me wrong, Dad and Mom are good at handling adult business. But it seems another family member is taking action in otherworldly fashion--rather than using legal--advocates.

It's not as though we're the most popular people in Babylon. Some Babylon folks have never accepted us. I've seen local folk cross the street when we're coming towards them. Some even make odd faces or shake a rabbit's foot at us. Evidently, all forms of "charms" have been used to keep us away; not to mention, the Jack Ketch knot, the shoot outs, the colored-basement treatment at the high school, Matteo's incident, the harassment at Danbee's, and any number of annoyances real and imagined.

What I hated most was my first shootout. Don't get me wrong; I'm glad it ended with zero people killed, but I can't tell anybody about it except--well, Bart. Not sure how I feel about the idea. Meanwhile, with all these nasty cowards around, I wouldn't be surprised to see a burning-cross in our front yard one day. But with Dad around, I feel sore sorry for anyone who tries.

Voodoo dolls and bones are the first sign I've ever seen of actual witchcraft being practiced on our land. Dad wastes no time, and in an afternoon of dirt, Horacio, Matteo and the big boys make the old root cellar a thing of the buried (but not forgotten) past. I can guess the culprit. But need a little help to investigate. When not terrorizing the place, Isabella lives in her room. Isaiah's swinging the yard stick is all the diversion I need to send Isabella into retreat as I search her room.

The idea of equal and enough seem to be turning around in my head. I think about Isabella's twin. I imagine one Isabella is enough. If she and her twin were together, I don't know what kind of trouble they might brew.

With Isabella chased out of the house, I act quickly. She is the only child with her own room. No one questions it. Generally speaking, no one wants to close their eyes too near her. It's not hatred but rather self-preservation. Something not too warm comes from her; like an easily avoidable iceberg no one wants to admit is dead ahead. Her museum-like organized room slows me down, but I know how not to move things. I especially know how to put them back, precisely, if I do move things. Her washcloth, clothes, even coat hangers all uniform, perfect, straight, all pointed in same direction, and aligned. The only item thrown willy-nilly is her filthy cloth doll. The doll is a token from her first birthday, which is the only comforting thing about Isabella; she's somewhat girly.

My snooping uncovers her 'girl cave' collection underneath the box-spring mattress frame. Isabella's storehouse of corn husks, matches, candles, small jars, pins, scraps of cloth and so forth. There is a list with 97 names on it; five of them are crossed out with deep red ink. At this point I'm thinking that whoever made the girl formula sugar and spice and everything nice, got the mix wrong where my sister is concerned! I take a few seconds to make sure I leave all the evidence, just like a smoking gun, exactly where I found it. Now what am I supposed to do?

CHAPTER 28
STORM FRONT

A few nights into April, the house and windows rattle like a doomsday disco-laser-light show. The storm is here. I discover quickly that prayer avails much, but as for what's left of hurricane Dorothy; it sure isn't in Kansas anymore. The tailwind, nowhere near its one-hundred-plus miles/per hour beginnings, is still enough to birth widespread flooding. Dorothy's tail end reaches Babylon and explodes until all at once (without being asked), the family piles in around the fireplace. I can't say why Hannah's children are still sleeping over, but the group joins our huddle.

The bunkhouse CB (citizens band) radio vibrating in words that Horacio (Horacio) sings out best. Matteo sounds off and I guess presses the microphone back into Horacio's hand. Horacio has no politics except that he loves the land and family, both for whom he labors faithfully. Like us, Horacio has his unfair share of authorities trying to twist, take, push, or shove him. I guess that's why he fits in so well. Horacio's and now Matteo's values line up with ours.

Dad and the bunkhouse radio squeal shot gun (but clear) Spanish. Later, I will be happy to repeat it all to Isabella for translation.

"Boys!" Dad commands as Luke, Peter and Paul stand ready. Dad turns his head "Get on your rain slickers; a tree has lodged in the watermill." The words launch three human missiles into a flurry of focus, fuss and motion, just as the CB blazes again.

"Bart to Booke. Come back. Over." Comes across in a throaty voice. "Bart to..." I feel a warm rush as Dad answers the CB in his sing-song Spanish. Black Bart replies in straight English.

"Your kids near huh? Oh. Over." It's the "oh" that brings the true heart frost. Dad continues the Spanish song and I understand enough to know that Black Bart's raw strength will be welcome, at least by me. Although welcome is not what my siblings may feel. Maybe the old creepy cold of electric spiders repelling down their spines is what they'll experience.

Bart hasn't done any of us ill, ever; but I used to feel so uneasy around him. Perhaps it's just our bias, his stealth, silence and strength all rolled together. I don't know. But now I just feel like he's well…he's just him, just a man, but maybe a bit more. I don't know how to say it when the monster becomes a mortal.

It's not logical, but it's there like that sound a house makes when it settles at night; then a perfectly safe and secure place is thrown into shades of sudden doubt. Bart is comfortingly nightmarish because he is the monster under the bed who's also on our side. Not surprisingly, Isabella is the only child not especially worried about this living shadow.

"I'm on my way. Over and out." Bart crackles over the radio as hope fades. In the pause, Isabella eyes me and shakes her head, acknowledging that our dark guardian is en-route.

"Honey," I hear Dad say softly to Mom. As I see Mom's smile, her eyes widen, and fists unclasp. "We're turning off the power at our mains to keep the winery temperatures and fermentation constant." He pauses and smiles. "Keep near the radio pack, batteries, and the portable. It's going to be a long night." The husband pauses and smiles at his wife. "I'll want good coffee," Dad continues. And for the first time in my lifetime, Dad kisses Mom in front of us all. All my sisters sigh in unison, then Ruth, Naomi and Rebecca hug each other.

Mom holds Dad for a silent moment her hand gently brushes down the side of his face; she nods and lets him go gather his gear. Moments later, the boys come rushing through, eagerly playing with their new walkie-talkies. They check their toys gleefully. Mom steps aside (only pressing a silver flask into Dad's pocket) as the horde of large Bookes men pour out into "the thunder, lightning and rain."

Against the hurly-burly, Mom draws the group close to her heart and the glowing fireplace. Somehow her arms feel like they fit around us all. Without effort, Mom makes humming into music. She and her soft voice rock us back and forth ever so sweetly, as her bodily sounds gather pitch, purpose and support. Each child joins in adding touches of joy. But Ruth, Naomi and Rebecca add their own heavenly "ah" as guide. Yet Mom directs effortlessly with "ooh" weaving our off sounds from uncertain grunts to peals of laughter and off pitch squeals into rich splashes of bliss.

Our joyful noise is praise to the Lord in gentle Holy Ghost tongues with no words but celestial oh, ah, ha, hum, and yah. Little by little, the thick-cold darkness all around us falls away. The warm light of Mom's heart hymnal brings peace to the still raging storm. One at a time, we drift into the lullaby, as even I drift off into a lovingly unplanned sleep.

CHAPTER 29
RUBBER MEETS THE ROAD

I wake naturally. For the first time in a long time, no
dreams! I guess my other selves didn't have anything bad to say.
Instead, I open my eyes to a cooling fireplace and the warm blaze
of a loved one's embrace. I pry myself from the puppy-pile of
heavily sleeping children. The hopeful smell of bacon, home fries,
pancakes, eggs, and such tempt my mouth. Though, it's still murky
dawn with darkness holding its last, I easily find the table.

"This is the best coffee you've made yet honey," Dad says
pressing the sloshing silver flask back into her hand. Mom smiles
as she 'purses' the flask. "Mr. Bookes," Dad greets me, "Did you
defend the house last night?" Dad asks.

"I did my best, Sir," I say drifting toward the pancakes.

"Then have a sip," Dad announces pushing the cup into my
hands. It's the first time my taste buds ever woke up instantly:
Irish-farmer's coffee. Now if I didn't have hair on my chest before,
I'm sure going to see some now! Suddenly, at this early hour, the
telephone rings. Mom answers it with, "yes, we're alright. We
weathered the storm," and so forth; but then, it keeps ringing and
Mom repeats the same statement over and over. Between the one-
sided phone calls and my new awareness, I hear the radio chatter
something about hurricane Dorothy's aftermath. The storm is over,
but the damage is far from done.

"Well, I'm glad to be here myself," Peter announces from
nowhere. "I fell into the river and washed right into your hands."
My blood turns cold hearing the responder.

"Glad to pull you from the deep," Bart's voice growls.
Only I seem to be stunned. The shadows of a corner turn into this
mountainous form. It doesn't help that Bart can't pronounce

certain lip sounds clearly. I figure any letter needing two lips to meet is a lost cause. "That log wasn't too friendly, neither" he continues as I translate his muddle speak.

"Joseph your Dutch-Uncle here did us proud last night," Dad says as I echo Dutch Uncle in the back of my head. Now at long last, I'm fine with my God-Uncle Solomon while Bart is now thought of as a phantom odd-father of doom.

"Dutch Uncle?" I blurt aloud.

"Well, yes. Bart's been your Dutch Uncle since your namesake Godfather, went missing back in '61," Dad says drawing suddenly silent over his own words and his steaming coffee. Dad almost never talks about certain relatives and this one, in my memory, never. Bart cuffs Dad's shoulder and brings him back into the moment; they chuckle. "Any way, Bart changed your diapers, more than once, too," Dad says. Without missing a beat, however, Dad turns on Bart. "By the way Bart, do you recognize this?" Dad asks pulling out a piece of black rubber.

"It looks like a rubber bullet," Bart says, taking it and twirling it between his fingers.

"Funny though, it looks like our old Crowd Control stock: Military Police Issue." Dad sips on his coffee, then continues. "I found this after that investigative photographer fellow had his camera shot clean out of his hands," Dad says, eyeing Bart. "Near as I can figure," Dad says, "that was one heck of a shot, considering the brush and line of sight issues," Dad ends with a coffee slurp. About then, the phone sings out again and Mom cups the mouthpiece.

"Phil, it's for you," Mom says to Dad.

"Saved by the bell," Bart says as Dad slides out of his chair to take the phone.

"Hello Sheriff…Yes, we're fine…Yup, our place is near 100%...Oh, sad to hear it…Oh, are you sure? I guess that'll be fine; it's the job…I reckon…We'll be ready," Dad says into the mouthpiece. He walks soberly to his chair and takes a long draught.

"Bart, we have some constitutionally certifiable quartering to do," Dad says, and I see Bart's outline wave.

"Wreak Havoc!" Bart calls out. Two shadows emerge from the darkness in the form of Doberman pinchers: exact twins of our dogs. Getting to the breakfast table, I --unawares-- walked right past them! Bart wheels himself around into the light, adjusts his bandanna over his lower face and steps up. "Slim, Slash," he croaks, and our two Doberman's bubble up. "Patrol!" Bart announces and in call order, the dogs march out of the room, through the door, then vanish into the shadows.

Dad doesn't move from his chair but rolls the coffee cup between his hands from palms to fingertips and back several times. I'm not sure what scares me most: dog invisibility skills, the sheriff's call, or this new appreciation of Bart!

Before I can rightly focus, the younger children swarm around the table; by the time I look up, plates are being served, the bigger folk are shuffling and just like the shadows that spawn-chaos; Bart is gone. I can't even recall hearing my Dutch Uncle move. It's an odd appreciation knowing just who is on my side.

Barely morning light, and Dad is chain sawing bunches of fallen trees, including the huge log which fouled our water mill. I imagine Peter, Paul and Luke are helping somewhere, because I can't see or hear them. Matteo and Horacio are working on the water and windmill: priming the generators. The little ones and me, we just handle whatever we can pick up, move, roll, or carry. The dogs and Bart are nowhere to be seen. There is no talk about it either. Dad's Range-Rifle, bullets and his police band radio sit on his porch bound rocking-chair.

Hours later, Dad's cautions become clear. A long white and brown bus labeled Fulbright Correctional Facility draws up to our gate. Four men in chains and one loose one, shuffle toward us from the vehicle. Dad waves at the bus driver and greets the inmates, a prison guard and the Sheriff as he opens wide our gate.

CHAPTER 30
THE THIRD AMENDMENT SIP

"This is temporary Deputy Bookes," Sheriff Witts says shaking Dad's hand, "until we sort out the storm damage." The Sheriff turns around but keeps talking; "This is Chief of the Guard, Wilson Mallory," he gestures, then introduces the well-muscled penitentiary officer.

"How do you do sir," Mallory says. The prisoners stand in a silent line. But one, the youngest, is all eyes. He doesn't move from the line but looks about the place and smirks.

"How do you do," Dad says shaking the Chief's hand.

"You understand the State and County will pay you a handsome fee and other compensations for quartering each inmate." Chief Mallory says, "We're staying true to our country's constitution in this matter," he continues with a glint of doubt in his eyes, as he looks over the place. "Sheriff Witts," continues Mallory, "has informed me of your unique qualifications." The young inmate makes a brief, fake coughing sound. Dad ignores it. "Are you sure you can handle these men?" asks Mallory.

"I've dealt with worse," Dad says staring at the youngest prisoner, "and, I understand the current code concerning reasonable conduct, accommodation and treatment, as well as the provision (if necessary) for extra-ordinary means." Dad says—still watching the youngest inmate.

"Oh," says Mallory a bit less concern in his voice. I guess the young prisoner is a concern. I imagine Dad will sort him out. He's good—and has had plenty of practice working with difficult young people; just ask my brother Luke.

"Mr. Bookes, I understand that you have a bunkhouse and another more secure facility? I'll need to inspect your facilities," says Mallory.

"Fair enough; I have the cooperage and its stone enclosed sub-basement. Mind you, it's about 15 degrees cooler than above ground. As to the bunkhouse, Mr. Greene will be the only inmate there," Dad says pointing to the non-encumbered jail bird. "Meanwhile, if the Sheriff can monitor these gentlemen, I'd be glad to show you the stone enclosed room, nine-inch-thick oak and steel re-enforced doors," Dad says as the same prisoner grunts; Sheriff Witts nods and unbuckles his pistol flap; off Dad and Mallory go.

Sheriff Witts is graying but has plenty of rust-free iron in his will. Not one of the prisoners dares to move. Their reflections in his mirrored sunglasses seem as motionless as our angel masthead poles at the entrance. The bugs have come out this early, but not in great number yet. There's still a sense that nature is waking up, though the birds have launched into their acrobatic business, before the bees.

Dad returns with rifle-toting Mallory, both are smiling. Handshaking, key giving, paper signing, head nodding, and off goes law enforcement. Dad sets down a plastic pail to his side.

"Have a seat, Mr. Green," Dad beckons the coughing fellow. Mr. Green, I should mention, has been coughing and hacking incessantly. He finds and fills the chair just behind where the prisoners are still standing.

"When will we get something to drink?" The young prisoner demands. Dad is unmoved. "Hey farmer, when do we get something to drink!" the young thug barks. Dad makes a bird call; a peculiar bird answers him. A moment passes.

"Slim, Slash, Reek, Havoc!" Dad hand signals, and all four Dobermans bolt towards him.

"What? Pestilence and Disease are somewhere else? The young prisoner laughs shakily.

"Death and Destruction," Dad bellows and two more dogs identical to Slim and Slash trot out and join the four others. Half a dozen Hades-hounds when one would do. Frowning, Dad points to each prisoner, "Post!" he blares as each dog stops in front of a different prisoner, except Mr. Green who has zero; guess who gets three points and three doggies?

"Son," Dad says to me.

"Yes sir," I reply.

"Have your sling shot and marbles?"

"I sure do."

"Well then, go ahead and peg that tin can from 20 feet." Dad commands and without a pause I fire and the can goes sailing from the stoop. "Right nice," he says as Slash growls at the shaken young thug.

"Young man, staying still is advisable." Dad advises the uppity prisoner. "Son!"

"Father," I say beginning to feel a game coming.

"Here," he pulls from the white plastic pail. "This is your compound sling shot and quarter inch ball bearings. Peg that cinderblock from that fence post. It has to be 30 feet," Dad commands: pointing. It takes me a few more seconds to aim, but the block shatters upon impact. "Good," Dad says rubbing my head. "You'll be carrying this and ball bearing from now on; no head shots this time please."

"Yes, I mean, no sir," I say nodding.

"Pick up a golf ball…good. Now fire it overhead." I do, and without a blink his pistol is outfired and the golf ball is flying chowder. "Son!"

"Yes sir," I say smiling.

"Watch," he says picking up three golf balls; he imitates another bird call then pauses; the birds answer. Dad calls again and a three-tweet echo is heard. Up the golf balls go and all three explode into chunks. Dad's pistol is still in its holster. Arms folded; Dad looks to the now especially quiet prisoners.

"Gentlemen, these dogs will be your guides. They'll teach you the boundaries. The dogs are Special Forces Sentry Hounds; their blood runs through three generations of military animals. Recently, their sire, Puck, was granted full military honors at Arlington and buried with his fallen field officer; one of a few for that hallowed ground gentleman. Some of these pups have worked before. Some will guard government facilities. Some will see duty in the new conflict in Southeast Asia. But right now, each one is here to watch you." Dad pauses to take a drink from his old canteen.

"They've got your scent. If they charge you, they don't stop unless commanded to "cease." They may a-t-t-a-c-k if you violate certain limits. I figure you're smarter than a dog so: learn!" Dad barks. "I am the only one with the 'stop/cease' command." Dad continues, "However, my entire family has the *"a-t-t-a-c-k strangers"* command. By-the-way gentlemen don't ever move too quickly or stand where there's another person between you and the dog or dogs guarding you. These pups will likely *a-t-t-a-c-k* instantly." Dad coughs and pauses for effect. "Again, they are here specifically to watch you. The word you should not use gentleman is spelled a-t-t-a-c-k unless you do not enjoy your life."

"In addition, the men all around us, that you can't touch, see, hear, smell, nor feel can easily taste your blood. They're all military. They will be the next generation of mixed special forces snipers. That means all branches of the military are represented here." Dad blows the thin whistle, and all six guard dogs attentively sit in front of our jail-bird guests. From behind, Dad walks up to and presses his old canteen up to the youngest thug's trembling lips.

"Shall we reason together?" Dad all but whispers.

CHAPTER 31
THE CHAIN GANG

They've had a long day. The inmates come home far too tired to cause a ruckus and with far too many reasons not to make trouble. In general, the prisoner's work is slow, heavy and boring. I can see the effort on each man's face: hard-heat and back-straining labor. The prisoners come in late and go out to work early. The chore of clearing flood damage and debris from the roadways is not one I'd want or wish on anyone. Because detail work cannot be done by machines, good old sweat of the brow is needed. Besides, I can see the Biblical wisdom of keeping 'these hands' busy and from becoming the devil's workshop. The prison bus collects our jailbirds after their breakfast, and except for Mr. Green, it takes them to some area, then returns them in the evening; tired, sweaty, dizzy, thirsty, and hungry.

Our dogs how no pleasure in greeting the inmates at their bus. The young prisoner (who has three dogs guarding him), is nowhere near as mouthy as he was. Mud-soaked through, they all jingle-march to the song of their ankle chains. Waiting at the bunkhouse, Mr. Green--shaking and coughing-- hands them a towel, soap, shampoo, and so forth. Dad unshackles them one at a time. Then the men stretch, straighten themselves, look at Dad, the dogs, the woods, and sometimes Dad again, only to enter the bunkhouse, followed by a canine. I hear the shower running, knowing each criminal is under devoted and watchful eyes.

Most of the girls and youngest family members, as well as Hannah's toddlers, are elsewhere. The problem is really Isabella: the youngest Bookes. You see, she is a Gemini, and you never know which twin --pardon the pun-- you're going to get: the evil one or the mischief-making one. It's a good thing she's going away with Aunt Clara. With lives at stake, Dad errs on cautioning by sending them away.

The inmates grumble a lot about their labor. I guess they should have read the Thirteenth Amendment (about the only form of legal slavery in the United States), before breaking the law. But no one complains about the fresh air, or the spacious bunkhouse. Least of all the complaints involve home-cooked meals, liberal with meat, biscuits, potatoes, pickles, and pies. Dinner is had with us on the pavilion or in the house. Dad holds daily prayer service. He hasn't left the place since the men arrived. To look at these convicts now showing no signs of the foul-mouthed hopeless cases they arrived as, now, hard-working souls. Not one moans of the sleeping arrangements or evening coolness of the sub-basement cooperage; not sure how they feel about kegs upon kegs of booze which their bare hands cannot open.

It's gotten so that several prison guards, not even on duty, stay for supper or overnight to watch the unique quartering at the Bookes' Detention and Wine Center. The politeness amazes the guards and the inmates amaze themselves, I'm sure. I don't suppose the guards know about Dad's woodland friends. The inmates don't seem to mention this point. I suppose the prison folk are curious as to why these jail birds haven't flown off.

Meanwhile, Matteo, who is still on the property, manages to be as ghost-like as the sharp shooters. The only difference is, I now and again get to see Matteo, once the prisoners are moved out in the morning. However, now that prisoners and twice as many guards visit, Matteo is almost always out of sight.

Just the same, Matteo enjoys his new bicycle liberally riding off every chance he gets. A couple of days ago, an inmate stepped close to being out-of-bounds and his post dog circled, displayed fangs, and herded him back. Dad paused to praise Slash and made a bird call. The tweet is returned several times over. The inmates then lowered their hopeless heads. They groaned, except Mr. Green, who doesn't seem to notice or care. No prisoner ever tempted fate again.

While the inmates are out, working day labor, Dad tries best he can to right our place. It's true the wind and water mill are working fine, but the winery needs constant attention. Dad checks the batch, measuring that one and adjusting kegs here and there. It's all work. I do his simple work of sprinkling the potty powder down the outhouse ports. I guess school being out for these several days isn't all rest and relaxation. Matteo is always home-schooling. We've taken him to the town hall library several times. But right now, he seems happy to stay here out of sight; though, this current level of invisibility is disturbing. Dad calls and calls for Matteo. Horacio and Mom can't find him, and we become concerned…well I do anyway. Dad just blows his wind whistle and calls one of the dogs. Death gets a whiff from Matteo's dirty laundry hamper.

"Seek!" Dad blurts and minutes later Death is scratching near the side porch of the house. Dad talks through the lath-board for a while but stops and comes to me.

"Go call Hannah. Ask her to get here; she's at the community center. "Dad says. I race into the house, inform Mom. She makes the call to Hannah, but I explain how Matteo is dug in under our porch like purple on a grape and how (right now), he needs her and so do we. Hannah gets to our place pretty quick, given the state of emergency. Dad greets her and points to the side porch. Without missing a beat, Hannah crawls right under the house. It's some time before there is any stirring. Matteo crawls from beneath the house, Hannah behind him. Dad smiles a thank you to Hannah. She acknowledges him by dusting off her jeans. Dad, with Matteo, walks off toward the empty bunkhouse.

"What's wrong?" I ask as Hannah puts her earring back in. She pauses and brushes my face gently with her hand.

"Nothing. He's just overwhelmed." Hannah says. "We have too many new faces and too much unwanted change." She sighs. "He don't like the inmates, guards, dogs, rifles, and them there 'ghost rifles:' whatever they is! He's just seen a lot."

"As much as you?"

"Yes, and more; you remember how I nearly jumped out of my skin the first time you surprise hugged me from behind?"

"Yes,"

"That startled feeling is what Matteo feels all the time...he's overwhelmed. It's called *shell shock*: a constant fear even when there is no real danger. Anyway, I need to talk to your Ma and Pa," Hannah says before walking away.

As I turn to watch Hannah go, I see Mr. Green looking on, sweating, shaking and drooling like a basket case vulture. He holds himself up, by the gate rail, watching; at standing, his labored breathing matches a marathon runner. Green can't be very old. His papers, I stole a look at, say he's younger than Dad. But Green is not a spring sapling either. Wayland, Green's first name, always looks like he's seasick. Even if he wants to run away, his ailment (whatever it is) would have him crashing at the gate.

"Poor kid," Mr. Green mutters about Matteo, I guess, and jarringly-rights himself to walk away. Mom, Dad and the dogs are at ease around him. However, I have as little to do with him or our other jailbird guests as possible. I feel a bit of what is (no doubt) eating at Matteo.

CHAPTER 32
"TWENTY-ONE GUN SALUTE"

"Who would believe it," starts Sheriff Witts while grilling the last of the steaks. "All those years ago, local government denials make them in your debt." He says to a satisfying sizzling sound. "They even refused to widen your dirty road," Witts sighs.

"Dad responds with one of my favorite quotes from the Bible: "As for you, you meant evil against me, but God meant it for good, to bring it about that many people should be kept."

"Amen!" I respond to a hearty set of chuckles.

"Well," continues the Sheriff, "they probably thought you'd fold without electric, water, septic, and refuse service; but look at this place! You're the only place to weather the storm. Your independence (down to your own generators) makes you strong."

"I don't know about all that," Dad says looking over all the guests (jailbirds and otherwise). "The religious Traddish Sect widened the dirt horse tracks to proper dirt roads, before they turned the deed over." Dad pauses to plate his steak.

"They sold us this land," he continues, "because they knew we would care for it. That's all; the roads, the water and windmill, the leach field as well as our cisterns, wells, reservoirs, the vineyards, and gardens come from God's grace, fulfilling our needs." Dad says to smiling faces.

"During this crisis, yours was the only place that didn't lose power, Phil. It's impressive," Witts says while slicing into a piece of beef, "and don't think I'll let the city fathers forget your gracious assistance." Sheriff Witts affirms and serves the first of a wave of sirloins.

Our prison guests have been clearing all kinds of storm damage; Dad's bunch is usually assigned to road, community, and local works. I'm sure the prisoners can't wait to return to their State provided home. Hopefully the other inmates have been as hard-working as Dad's squad. The eight days of temporary housing were good for the prisoners who seem used to their canine leashes; the dogs themselves sit suspiciously, still eyeing their charges with 'a watch you or eat you' attitude. I suppose the prisoners are more relaxed here than anywhere else. They seem like they're happy.

Dad still refuses to have any of the girls (except Mom and Hannah) around. Matteo stays with Mom and Hannah in the house. He has less to do with the 'policia' as he calls them. He's even nervous around Dad sometimes. I guess the Auxiliary Sheriff badge makes Pa 'policia' too. Uniforms, guns, dogs, and nightsticks bother him. Dad gives Matteo space and does not press him. Before my "treaty with my inner selves," Dad could sit near my bed at night and scare away my monsters, but Matteo's demons are of a different sort. He and Hannah have similar wounds caused by what I imagine to be a similar evil. I suppose Matteo will open up to her soon enough. I know that holding fears in causes nothing but pain. Not to mention how it eats away at you. Peaceful sleep does not come during night terrors. I can't imagine the lack of comfort that exists with actual day terrors.

Although I'm not sure what these prisoners are sentenced with, I follow Dad's cautious wisdom. I don't like the idea of harming anyone, but I know I can hurt any one of these guys if they get stupid. I'm not so sure about the women's abilities. But I know Dad doesn't really feel like choking the life out of anyone; but if the need arises, I'm certain his hands are more than capable.

The prisoners fill the table left and the guards sit facing them long table right. They laugh and relate storm repair tales.

Several odd tasks turned out to be rescues. It seems that in pumping out basements quite a few pets were recovered alive and well. Cats and dogs and other critters seem to hide on the highest part of basement rafters. The youngest prisoner chuckles as the older ones tease him about the elderly couple hugging and kissing him. I believe there is actually a glistening in the corner of his eye. All seem pleased about something. The prisoners are likely pleased that they are working right now. The local government is glad that the inmates cleared trees, moving downed power-line poles, towing vehicles, and a host of other needed tasks.

"Phil, I just don't know what this county would have done without you," Sheriff Witts continues. Dad just nods and passes corn to the fellows. Mom and Hannah are in the house with Mr. Green. I hear Green's ever-present cough. Matteo, like our snipers, remains out of the prisoner's and guard's sight. The prisoners recently (at last) stopped harassing Mr. Green about hacking up half a lung daily, then growing a new 'promethean replacement' overnight, only to hack it out again. I am surprised by their story reference. I guess prisoners have plenty of time to read. Green keeps to himself, like Matteo. If not for his call sign coughing, I'd barely notice him. He's worn out and torn down by something I pray I never see. His coughing is one thing, but his sadness is almost palpable. I mean his body carries "the scars of much experience," as Horacio would say. I scan the yard with hopes of finding our migrant-ramrod. Horacio doesn't leave at the end of the season. Unlike most of our helpers, Horacio is a permanent fixture like a thick paint on the wall which "covers a multitude of sins."

"We must get ready for tomorrow," Witts says.

"That can wait Sheriff," Dad says as he stands, gestures, and blows the wind whistle. The dogs move to the head of the table and sit. We finish the meal, clear the table from one side as the prisoner's smoke cigarettes. The dogs position themselves at table head and watch the inmates intently.

"Joseph, take this," Dad hands me a platter for Mr. Green, "and go into the house," Dad instructs me. I feel his trickery coming. You need to understand that until this point, Dad has let me be right in the thick of things. I've known all the doings. But not this time. Dad dismisses me. On my way, I see Matteo's hand from beyond the side-porch corner. I turn to see Dad watching me go into the house. Mom and Hannah receive the tray and spread the table. Mr. Green sleeps in Dad's recliner. Mom will call us when it's time. However, it's a moment or so before I steal to the side window. Matteo enters, "like a thief in the night."

"They leave tomorrow," Matteo says eyeing Mr. Green. "And I say good riddance!"

"I reckon the flood and storm damage has been cleared?"

"I do not know. I sleep better without them!" Matteo says. As I sigh, I note the dirty stains on Matteo's knees and elbows. I imagine he's sleeping away from the bunkhouse: probably under the side porch.

"Good enough," I say reaching up to his shoulder. Matteo's smile is short lived.

"Your Dad trusts too many bad men," Matteo says before he goes, washes up and joins Hannah and Mom in the kitchen. Since I've eaten, I wait quietly watching Mr. Green's labored chest rise and fall between each breath.

The next morning the prisoner's bus arrives with little fanfare. And shackle-less Mr. Green is numbered among them. He trembles even in the gentlest breeze. Dad and dogs have the prisoners at the gate. Matteo, for the first time in days, stands in plain sight with guards and prisoners around. His knees are still soiled and there is a trembling to his steps. Sheriff Witts and the Chief of the Guard stand ready with no weapons out, but keen eyes studying all.

One at a time, the full set of prisoners with chain-locked hands, feet and ankles arrive. Dad blows his wind whistle and points to each dog and each prisoner. "Release!" he commands. One at a time the dogs become instantly distracted and wander off to the shade, shadows, or some part of the yard. Dad waits with the youngest prisoner. The young man seems like the saddest one as the dogs trot off.

"I almost wish I could stay," he says to Dad. Dad smiles and presses a Bible into the young man's hands.

"You'll be done with your sentence one day," Dad says in a way of encouraging.

"Well, I'm glad we're done with the dogs and those snipers. You never fooled me. You only have a fellow or two out there." The uppity prisoner says as Dad's eyes cut into him. "But it was a mighty good bluff," the young prisoner quickly says thumbing his new Bible.

"A fellow or two," Dad repeats. "Good luck son; to all of you." As the group shuffles toward the bus, Dad twists the tube on the long wind whistle. The bus door closes. The driver loops in the turn around and stops. Dad walks to the bus door with Chief of the Guard Mallory

"Thank you, Mr. Bookes," Mallory says while pressing a thick envelope into Dad's hand. "Sign here," he says handing him a clipboard. "I think it only fair that you not have to wait for payment; you provided exemplary service to the State sir. I believe you'll find this compensation acceptable." Mallory continues: "On a personal note, I loved the power of suggestion. You kept the prisoners guessing. I just wish you did have an army surrounding them." Mallory sighs. "You took quite a risk," he says, "but I understand the Sheriff's confidence in you." Dad smiles, turns sharp face-right and shouts.

"Boo-rah!"

"Boo-rah!" echoes back many times above nature's sounds. Woodland leaves, branches and flowers shake into rough human form as dozens of sharp shooters flank the bus. I go and stand near Dad watching, as the Sheriff and lastly the sharp shooters fade into the distance and/or woods, each and of their own. Matteo trips over himself in retreat. I press my hand against my racing heart and hidden cross.

Mr. Green is still in our yard!

CHAPTER 33
COME JOIN THE FIGHT

"You have to understand, Mr. Bookes, Matteo's condition was nearly fatal," Young Dr. Siegel Jr. declares." It's rare that I need to give an adolescent a full ice-bath," Doc wipes his brow. "It's rarer still to play catch-up on years of prophylactic regimens as well; not to mention the dental care Matteo still requires. I wish you would have come months ago." Doc wrings his bag handle in his hands, before looking up to continue. "But as it is, I had to report the 'seeming neglect' or potentially lose my license. I'm sorry." Doc's eyes glisten but do not water our gate.

"I don't fault you and am grateful." Dad says.

"For some reason, the Babylon Health Department--although not directly involved--is extremely interested in this case," Doc says. Dad sighs. I'm sure the Sovereign Sausage Inc. Brummun clan will use whatever means it can to get this land or at a minimum mess with us. "Well," continues Doc, "until social services and child protective can sort this out, he's yours. But my advice, if I may?" Doc pauses and makes firm eye contact with Dad. "Get Matteo's original birth certificate and any other documentation, before Immigration and the Feds gets involved."

"I understand." Dad says, shaking hands and gathering up Matteo's new prescriptions.

We had a real scare last week when Matteo's eyes were swollen shut and he looked like a brow-beaten prize fighter. According to Doc, some thorns (raspberry cane), were stuck as deep as bone level and rotted. It took a while, but Matteo went into septic shock. It doesn't help that Matteo has no regular medical anything. Why the list of shots, treatments, tests, and appointments almost makes me glad to have mine all spread out. But Matteo--by necessity if not design-- is tough as steel.

"That was nice of John Jr." Dad says, sorting the medical scripts. "He didn't have to drive out here to follow up on Matteo."

"I reckon not," I say.

"I guess runaways don't get regular check-ups," Dad says with a pained smile.

"Burocrata clinica!" I reply and Dad rests his hand upon my crown. "What'll happen now?" I ask.

"We fight." Dad says staring into the distance and an invisible foe. "Young Mr. Bookes we fight" he repeats.

Dad has Matteo—vaccine pin-cushion extraordinaire resting in the main house. Shaking to tears, Matteo had no say in his recent hospital stay. He went days with his jaws swollen shut, which afforded him even less of a voice. Now that he can speak, he doesn't; mostly, he just stares at our ceiling.

It's a few days of 'Burocrata' swimming around our place; Child Protective, Social Service, the Health Department. Each group with a bunch of charges and alleged abuse claims, which Dad responds to with calm, clear, legal counsel. God-Uncle Solomon is earning his keep. He is throwing legalese to a high degree of fertilizer perfection. He, Dad, Bart, and Horacio fend off these unusual attackers. But, Matteo, like the Apostles in that stormy boat, does not find peace nor can he be still.

"I have to go," Matteo says rising a little only to have the gravity of his situation fail him again. "I will not go back to the whorehouse!" unable to rise, Matteo turns himself toward the door as tears spill. "Your family will lose everything, everything if I stay! I'm not worth it. They…they..." For a moment, he falls silent unable to get out another word. I turn and see Mr. Green, not coughing, walking past the open doorway. Wild-eyed Matteo grips my arm. "I cause much trouble for your family. Maybe, as Horacio said, we can't win all battles." He pauses to add snot to the flow of tears and saliva. Damp cloth in hand, I wipe until his face is his own again.

Mom, Hannah, Rebecca, Naomi, and Ruth react with surprise to Matteo's outburst. He's not ranting from fever. Matteo is rational. Yesterday morning, Hannah says, "Long ago, that one time when you surprise hugged me, you remember how I nearly jumped out of my skin? That loving hug you gave me was so long gone from my life that I didn't trust it. For just a moment, I couldn't accept that other people could care for me. I couldn't let myself be open and vulnerable. That's Matteo, right now. I reckon he loves what he's getting from you all, but he's even more afraid it'll be destroyed because of him." As if that makes sense: fear of family? Anxiety or not, Matteo is safe, even with the newest ghost Green present. Nothing bad will happen. Though Dad doesn't take time to explain Mr. Green's situation or why he's still here.

A day passes and Matteo is strong enough to rise. A few more days and he can get out of bed on his own. Except for the hovering of motherly hens, Matteo is much better. Mom and Hannah, watch over him with loving parent-like care. I seldom see our guest room so well used. Both Doc Siegel Jr. and Doc Siegel Sr. pay Matteo a call. And just as expected, a form of the old snake shows up to serve more legal papers.

The yard has no ghost warrior sharp shooting from the shadows; our regular two dogs stand attentive, but with no enemy. Luke stealthily films the papers being served to Dad in Super 8 Extended format. Luke--has fallen in love with the camera! Unarmed Dad receives the snake's skin, handed to him over the closed gate; he reads the legal paperwork without budging from his post.

Dad reaches into his pocket and sheds skin of his own. He's counter-serving papers to the server! I recognize the yellow - envelope Dad pushes over the closed gate. I know it contains a legal paper. God-Uncle Solomon's counteraction to the snakes' paper is a work, no doubt, expertly done.

The worker, whoever he is, a waiting ambulance and two State Police look over Dad's paper. A few moments pass and grudgingly, they all turn and leave empty handed. I didn't hear a word but know that that's one tactic the enemy won't try again. Dad smiles and returns to Mom's yard project.

The family fans out about the vineyard. Mom, after setting up all the other particulars, dawns her lye soap-making gear. She needs to make a three gross (144X3) order of lavender homespun. The Traddish are excellent customers, but mighty particular about their orders. Dad tries his best to look busy, while 'happening' to be near Mom. It's about as accidental as Isaiah and I 'happening' to be around cookies in the oven and licking mixing spoons that 'happen' to be there. Mom doesn't send her 'audience' away. Making raw lye from the birch ash and then combining it with liquid fat is tricky. Mom's oil of choice is strained kitchen grease. She has a large free supply thanks to Danbee's Restaurant grease traps. The problem is, if you mix this stuff wrong, let's just say lye can poison, burn, spray, or blow-up in your face. It's almost as safe as milling your own dynamite! If I did Mom's job, I know I'd be counting my fingers at the end of each day. A few hours into the day I discovered that lye soap isn't the only violent process bubbling.

"I must go! Matteo screams as I wade in. Matteo is swinging wildly to break free. Mr. Green is a sweat, foul, bloody mess with a Mexican looped in his arms.

"No!" Green hollers back. Stunned, I run toward them only to stand staring.

"No! You're not running away! Hit me as hard as you like, I won't let go!" Matteo writhes, twists and pulls without letting up. Green holds like an anchor in the storm.

"Matteo, you are running the wrong way!" Green coughs, horribly bound to the young Mexican. "Running from help." He says whipping Matteo around. "These people were once my enemies and rescued me!" Green hollers through his own tears, snot, and blood. "I'm a no-good thief dying of lung cancer! I can't say I don't deserve better. I got nothing and nobody. But I'm not running away; not this time. No! Mr. Bookes done knocked me out; he jailed me, got me time served…compassionate release; he set me free," Green says trembling, speaking, and wrestling: even with his prayer. "His family is willing to see I get taken care of until the end and then buried decent too." Green raises his head to receive an elbow for his trouble. "Mr. Bookes had to knock sense into me too." Green lifts Matteo over a shoulder but the wriggling youth falls back to a standing hold. "I got nothing and nobody. I run out on them; run nowhere. Lord, help me! Boy, can't you see! Keep hitting me, I ain't lettin' go! I'm not lettin' you end up with my old life: alone. Oh, Lord help me! I done wrong in my life, Father God, much wrong; and if keeping this boy here from runnin' kills me, then I die today!" Green's arm almost gave way for a second, but he clamped down again. "You wrong boy! I won't let you run! I won't. Lord my arms! Please no, don't let them fail. No! You got two of Moses' helpers holding up that rod for battle…"

I move without pause gripping Matteo with Isaiah, Isabella, Naomi, Paul, Luke, and the others; and before I know it, Hannah, her children, Dad, Horacio, and Solomon encircle us: holding us all together. There is no weakness when the Bookes family stands together and we stand up the most when trouble is tallest.

Even after we let go, we stand strong. Mr. Green and Matteo hold each other in the center of a crying, laughing, unbreakable family embrace. It may have taken a criminal wrestling his conscience to stop an ill-fated orphan, but it will take the whole family to win this upcoming battle.

I'm heartened for the ongoing raging of this war.

ABOUT THE AUTHOR

Hollis Phillips is a martial artist, youth advocate and urban educator, who delights in working with city kids. He likes to point out that they are as likely to hug you one moment as they are to curse you the next. For three decades, Mr. Phillips has helped young people to, as the saying goes, "[not] turn your feelings into felonies." He assists youthful scholars navigate raw and unsettling situations.

Similarly, his fiction reflects the same gritty, inevitable and endearing qualities about an individual's ultimate societal power: choice and voice.

TURN THE PAGE FOR AN EXCEPT FROM THE NEXT PART OF THE BOOKES FAMILY ADVENTURES SERIES, COMING SPRING OF 2026

1

BOOK 2

"THE RAID IS THE RAGE"

I'm fast asleep, which is a good thing at midnight. Thunder rolls through the house, flashing lightning and an odd emptiness. There are three parts to a summer storm: thunder, lightning and rain. This one is somehow incomplete.

Even in my sleep there should be soothing raindrops prancing against roof tiles. Half-conscious, the crash rouses me...

Life has not begun until a SWAT team tosses your house! There is nothing as exciting as a fully armed nightmare. Public enemy number one, Dad, leaves every light on in the house--all night long-- for several days. I understand it now. Christmas tree style, we are backlit. In other words, through every window in the place, anyone can see us perfectly, but we can't see them. During the first raid the cops drove up to the front and bathed the house in headlights. There is frantic door-knocking but no battering rams, no flash-grenades, nor sharp shooters. Their reasonable requests become our lawful response. Apparently, our woodland ninja-elves didn't attack.

The State Troopers are all business. At 12:05 a.m., they find Matteo (well fed and cared for), sleeping alone; not beaten, cold, and wet lying in a dirty pit as the anonymous source had reported to Child Protective Services. Secretly, Luke is running his Super 8 camera. He wedges it on in a corner, at an angle. It might have been nice if the Troopers hadn't found it and turned it off. We all got frisked and searched for weapons: the boys and girls separated. At first, they were sort of grumpy, but after an hour they were nicer. The first raid is more like a ghetto fire drill. Now the second raid for illegal drugs is a hoot.

Raid two, the Troopers bring dogs: frisk and search, separate and storm. Not as nice about putting everything back. Evidently, the new complaint against us involves illegal drugs. We are up, out and in front of our house. Their dogs go up and down, through all structures, sniff, sniff, and sniff. No illegal discovery.

"Sir, rein your dogs!" a Trooper says to Dad. It seems that Slim and Slash (without being bidden) position themselves between the officers and the girls.

"If you think that'll be necessary." Dad says to the nervous cop. Dad blows his dog whistle and to the Trooper's horror, most of the police raid dogs immediately swarm my father. Dad spins around and kneels at the center of a canine-lick storm. As it turns out, Dad was most of the animals' primary trainer.

Raid three, the Troopers leave their dogs back. It may as well be a picnic. There are no wide-eyed police waiting for some shootout either. This time, they arrive as lambs.

"Is somebody after you?" a now familiar State Trooper asks.

"[He is] prowling like a roaring lion seeking whom he may devour," Dad says, handing out hot chocolate. The Troopers evaluate and walk the place quickly…slurping.

"Well, Satan notwithstanding, it doesn't seem like you have an illegal stockpile of weapons." The Trooper returns the unloaded range rifle to the new glass cabinet in the front room. "I'm impressed. Your place is astounding sir," the Trooper shares enjoying his second hot chocolate. "I don't know why they keep sending us."

"Thank you; I don't know either. But this is the cleanest the place has been since Christmas," Dad declares, as Mom cuffs the back of his neck; everyone laughs. But somehow, I remember an ancient Chinese curse Uncle Solomon likes to quote "may people in high positions take special interest in your welfare." In other words, life is good now, but things can easily (and probably will) get worse.

www.ingramcontent.com/pod-product-compliance
Lightning Source LLC
Chambersburg PA
CBHW030333020726
47493CB00004B/1260